# Credits

<table>
<tr><td>

**Author**
John M. Stater

**Developers**
Bill Webb

**Producer**
Bill Webb of Necromancer Games

**Editor**
Bill Webb of Necromancer Games

**Layout and Production**
Charles A. Wright

**Front Cover Art**
MKUltra Studios

</td><td>

**Interior Art**
Rowena Aitken

**Cartography**
Robert Altbauer

**Playtesters**
Frog God Games Staff

**Special Thanks**
Bill Webb would like to thank Bob Bledsaw and Bill Owen for inventing the original hex crawl — the standard in wilderness adventure and a lifetime of fun.

</td></tr>
</table>

FROG
GOD
GAMES

TOUGH
ADVENTURES
FOR TOUGH
PLAYERS

# Table of Contents


Beyond the Black Water .......................................................................... p. 4
Rumors .................................................................................................... p. 6
Encounter Key ........................................................................................ p. 6
— Hexes 0105, 0109 ............................................................................... p. 6
— Hexes 0113, 0116, 0122, 0202, 0210, 0218 ....................................... p. 8
— Hexes 0301, 0321, 0408, 0414 .......................................................... p. 9
— Hexes 0414, 0502, 0505, 0512, 0520, 0609 ....................................... p. 10
— Hexes, 0612, 0713, 0716, 0719, 0804 ............................................... p. 11
— Hexes 0810, 0818, 0822, 0921 .......................................................... p. 12
— Hexes 1007, 1015, 1019, 1102, 1112 ................................................. p. 13
— Hexes 1209, 1217, 1305, 1313, 1322 ................................................. p. 14
— Hexes 1401, 1407, 1502, 1515 .......................................................... p. 15
— Hexes 1520, 1612, 1703, 1706 .......................................................... p. 16
— Hexes 1711, 1913, 2004, 2009, 2108 ................................................. p. 17
— Hexes 2111, 2121, 2205 .................................................................... p. 18
— Hexes 2303, 2308, 2405, 2409 .......................................................... p. 19
— Hexes 2415, 2511, 2603, 2607 .......................................................... p. 20
— Hexes 2618, 2713, 2716, 2804, 2810, 2903 ....................................... p. 21
— Hexes 2914, 3017, 3101, 3109, 3113 ................................................. p. 22
— Hexes 3120, 3204, 3402, 3407, 3413 ................................................. p. 23
— Hexes 3517, 2521, 3609, 3802, 3805 ................................................. p. 24
— Hexes 3815, 3821 .............................................................................. p. 25
New Monsters .......................................................................................... p. 26
Legal Appendix ...................................................................................... p. 28

# Hex Crawl Chronicles

## — Beyond the Black Water —

### By John M. Stater

Among the reasons many adventurers choose to end their days in the cannibal-ridden, hurricane-savaged isles of the south is the immense distance it puts between them and the terrible land beyond the Black Water. The Black Water is a great inland sea filled with black, viscous water that sits as still as death. Nobody but a fool would willingly cross the Black Water, save for the strange men who sail the black arks, but many fools have crossed those waters in search of a lost love or a secret taken to the grave, for beyond the Black Water and its grey shores lies the icy Land of the Dead.

Though many a desperate man has sailed the Black Water and set foot on its noisome shores, only a handful have returned to speak of what they saw, and then only on their death beds. Some sages have such a testament in their possession to wonder over in the bright light of day. The scrolls tell of jagged peaks and white forests, spongy lake lands and black rivers, of barges stacked with corpses and a brisk trade in souls. Of the men who live in this land, they have been called "the beyonders", little is written or known, for they are not a talkative people and one does not easily extract themselves from their hospitality.

What, then, wanderer of worlds, plunderer of tombs, slayer of dragons, do you seek in the land beyond the Black Water? A departed friend or lover, an enemy who took the ultimate escape to avoid your wrath or a secret sealed behind the shriveled lips of a dead man? More importantly, how do you plan to return?

Beyond the Black Water is a hex-crawl, referring to the hex-shaped units that divide the map. Just as dungeon adventures take place on a gridded map, wilderness adventures can be conducted on a hex map, allowing players the freedom to decide where their characters roam and giving them the thrill of discovering the many places and people that have been placed on the map. This map represents a large area filled with numerous places to discover and explore, and can be used as a campaign area in its own right, or dropped into an existing campaign. Referees can place adventures they have purchased or devised on their own into empty hexes on the map.

## Adventures in the Wilderness

The Land Beyond the Black Water is both of the mortal world and beyond the mortal world, a nexus of the lands of life and death. The country is always shrouded in twilight, with a moon that rises and sets in the manner of the sun in the land of the living. The souls of the dead wash up on the land's rocky shores as spirits made corporeal and trapped in lifeless bodies. Some float up the river, for the Sluggish River flows from the sea to the mountains, rather than the reverse. Some souls animate their fleshy prisons in the form of zombies, others escape as ghostly shadows and many are extracted and traded as commodities by the weird citizens of this terrible country. Zombies and shadows instinctively make their way north, as baby sea turtles instinctively head towards the sea after hatching, for beyond the jagged Badlands is the Earthbound Paradise. Those souls that are captured or make their way up the river without escaping their bodies are claimed by the Nine Petty Deaths, the self-proclaimed regents of this land. All the lords and ladies of the land beyond the Black River serve the Nine Petty Deaths save the beyonders, who know their true nature.

The hexes on this map are 6 miles wide from one side to the other. In open country, adventurers should be able to see from one side of the hex to another. In wooded hexes, vision is much more restricted. Random encounters with monsters should be diced for each day and each night, with encounters occurring on the roll of 1-2 on 1d6. The exact monster (or monsters) encountered depends on the terrain through which the adventurers are traveling. Unlike dungeons, in which the monsters on the upper levels are usually less powerful than the monsters on deeper levels, wilderness encounters are quite variable in their challenge, and low level characters face death every time they step out of the confines of civilization. Well traveled adventurers will discover, however, that settled lands are not as dangerous as the rugged wilderness.

## The Land Beyond the Black Water

The black arks are tall galleys with three levels of oars but lacking sails. As one might imagine, they are constructed from black wood, sealed with tar and equipped with rams of black bronze. The arks are rowed by untiring zombies and crewed by the mysterious beyonders. The beyonders are tall and hunched. They wear layers of gauzy black robes, veils and turbans and take great pains to keep their hands hidden. Beyonders always carry curved blades at their sides. Some say that they

| Roll | Black Water | Badlands | Gray Steppe | Noisome Moor | White Woods |
|---|---|---|---|---|---|
| 1 | Black Ark (1) | Ogre (1d4+2) | Patrol (Necrophages) | Giant Centipede (1d6) | Orc (2d6+3) |
| 2 | Ghoul (2d6+6) | Patrol (Embalmers) | Centaur (1d4+3) | Orc (2d6+3) | Dryad (1d4) |
| 3 | Locathah (3d6+6) | Zombie (1d2) | Giant Ant (1d6+5) | Zombie (2d4) | Giant Boar (1d6) |
| 4 | Narwhale (1d4) | Shadow (1d2) | Giant Hyena* (1d6+2) | Shadow (2d4) | Zombie (1d4) |
| 5 | Nixie (3d6+6) | Wights (1d3) | Ghul (1d6+6) | Ghouls (1d6) | Shadow (1d4) |
| 6 | Sea Serpent (1) | Ghouls (1d4+2) | Shadow (1d4) | Patrol (Swampers) | Wolf (2d6) |
| 7 | Troll (2d6) | Ghasts (1d3) | Wolf (2d6) | Ghasts (1d3) | Giant Owl (1d4) |
| 8 | Zombie (3d6+6) | Giant Lemur (1d6)* | Zombie (1d4) | Shambling Mound (1d4) | Black Bear (1d6) |

* Treat giant lemurs as baboons and giant hyenas as worgs.

are zombies, ghouls or demons beneath their robes, others that they are merely shriveled, hideous humans. Most black arks carry two or three of the beyonders and a complement of thirty skeleton warriors armed with spears and longbows. Each beyonder on a black ark can cast spells as a cleric of level 1st to 6th and magic-user of level 1st to 4th.

# Black Arks

The black arks are tall galleys with three levels of oars but lacking sails. As one might imagine, they are constructed from black wood, sealed with tar and equipped with rams of black bronze. The arks are rowed by untiring zombies and crewed by the mysterious **beyonders**. The beyonders are tall and hunched. They wear layers of gauzy black robes, veils and turbans and take great pains to keep their hands hidden. Beyonders always carry curved blades at their sides. Some say that they are zombies, ghouls or demons beneath their robes, others that they are merely shriveled, hideous humans. Most black arks carry two or three of the beyonders and a complement of thirty skeleton warriors armed with spears and longbows.

# Ochre Rains

Ochre rain is thick and yellowish-brown and there is a 1 in 6 chance per day of it falling from the sky. It leaves a sticky, tarry substance on the skin which, if not quickly washed away with fresh water, raises lesions on the skin. These lesions reduce one's charisma and constitution by 1d6 points (half that with a successful save vs. poison), the abilities healing at the rate of 1 point per week. In the days after an ochre rain, a race of short-lived toadstool men emerges from the ground. These toadstool men are like malevolent children, roaming in packs of 3d6 individuals and causing all the havoc they can in the few days they have life. They are misshapen, with mismatched limbs, wide coral-colored caps spotted white and pinched, wrinkled faces with deep, slit mouths that emit a poisonous breath (see New Monsters for more information). Encounters with these toadstool men occur on a daily roll of 1-3 on 1d6 the day after the ochre rain falls. This roll is made in addition to normal random encounter rolls.

# The Nine Petty Deaths

The nine petty deaths are chthonic godlings that fancy themselves the archons of the land beyond the Black Water. They dwell in strongholds in the Badlands and gather at a grand tower [2205] with nine entrances to lay claim to the souls of the departed that have been captured in this land before they could travel to the Earthbound Paradise. Each petty death has his or her retinue, court functionaries and regalia and each death despises the others. They often capture souls claimed by their fellows to enable them to make cannier trades for more valuable souls. All of the lords and ladies of the land beyond the Black Water except the beyonders pay fealty to one petty death or another, with alliances shifting daily. The beyonders respect the power of the petty deaths, but know their true nature and so decline to pay them tribute. The nine petty deaths are: Atoda **(Hex 2004)**, Egygddedrol **(Hex 2607)**, Emntrix **(Hex 3204)**, Gohl **(Hex 0502)**, Heruldos **(Hex 0301)**, Ingueas **(Hex 1102)**, Lewl **(Hex 1401)**, Uddeso **(Hex 3402)** and Wihiedro **(Hex 3101)**.

# Men

The principal human cultures of the land beyond the Black Water are the beyonders (the pilots of the Black Arks), embalmers, necrophages and swampers.

**Beyonders** are human, but not wholly human (see New Monsters below). They are never seen unrobed, which is fortunate for all involved since they are tall and hunched, with ghastly, hairless skin and leering yellow eyes. They grow their finger and toe nails quite long and decorate their bodies with triangular metal charms hung on chains that pierce their flesh. As mentioned above, beyonders are always wrapped in multiple layers of clothing – cloaks over robes over tunics, etc. They wear dark, morose colors and always wear curved swords and daggers hanging from chain shoulder harnesses. The beyonders value secrets above all things, trading in secrets and knowledge the way others trade in coins and gems. In fact, coins and gems are not used at all by the beyonders and found treasures of this kind are casually cast away by them. Instead, one purchases things from a beyonder by telling them secrets – the more dire the secret and the more powerful person it is about, the more the secret is valued. Beyonders might pay adventurers in rumors or secrets germane to a Referee's campaign.

The **Embalmers** are a race of bronze skinned men with raven hair and violet eyes. They are short and stocky, the women voluptuous and the men given to wide exaggerations and long melancholies. Male embalmers dress in woolen tunics and trousers and gray cloaks. They wrap their lower legs in leather thongs and wear leather sandals on their feet and intricately patterned conical wool caps on their heads. Women wear loose gowns, a wide leather belt wrapped just under their breasts, shorter cloaks and put their hair in braids. Warriors arm themselves with spear, shields of wood and leather, short bows and long knives. The embalmers raise sheep, trading wool and foodstuffs for fragrant oils and herbs used in their embalming ritual, the aspect of their culture which gives it its common name. The embalmers make mummies of their dead philosophers and nobles, walling them into their temples and palaces that they may advise future generations through barred windows. Peasant corpses are burned for heat in the furnaces of their palaces. Embalmer patrols may be encountered on horseback (2 in 6 chance), in which case they are also armed with long hammers. An embalmer patrol consists of 2d6+4 men-at-arms led by a 3 HD sergeant.

The **Necrophages** are fierce warriors who roam the rolling steppe with their herds of cattle, riding in war chariots. The necrophages consume the flesh of their dead and of enemy casualties in war. They are berserkers in combat, wear leather and ring armor, carry shields, leaf-bladed short swords, spears and javelins and make use of scythe-wheeled chariots drawn by giant hyenas. While one might expect berserkers to charge into combat screaming, the necrophages fight in perfect silence. Clerics cast *silence* on the tribe's war chariots, so that their charging armies make almost no sound as they sweep across a battlefield. Necrophages are tall and lean, with pallid skin that they paint in grotesque patterns using burgundy paint made from crushed elderberries and columbines. Necrophage tribes are ruled by undead kings, wights, with worthy challengers raised by force of will when they die to challenge the existing wight-king. The necrophages worship Emntrix, the petty death who claims the souls of soldiers. A necrophage patrol consists of 1d6x3 men-at-arms in war chariots (3 in a chariot, a driver, a spearman and a longbowman) pulled by 2 giant hyenas (treat as worgs).

The final human culture in the land beyond the Black Water is the **Swampers**, or swamp folk. The swamp folk are albinos with long, kinky hair that they sculpt into a shape reminiscent of large horns or cones. They have broad faces and large, pink eyes. The swampers dress in soft leather tunics and the more accomplished hunters wear black cloaks made from the pelts of swamp panthers. Swampers encountered outside their villages are hunters or gatherers looking for exotic herbs and insects. The gatherers carry horn-handled sickles, often silver bladed, leather slings, wicker holy symbols, spirit rattles and bags of herbs, including healing poultices (+1 hit point healed per night) and bundles meant to repel the undead (as a *scroll of protection from undead*). Spirit rattles are made from a variety of floating gourd with noxious flesh. These gourds are emptied and hollowed and filled with corpse teeth and allow a skilled swamper to turn undead as a 1st level cleric, though undead that would be effected by this turning can make a saving throw to resist. Gatherers are usually accompanied by a breed of large, white swine that are used as mounts, pack animals and to sniff out herbs and funguses. A swamper village consists of a number of stilt-houses, separated from the other houses of the village by an average of 100 yards and lit with lamps fueled by corpse oil. These "corpse lights" foil invisibility, especially the invisibility enjoyed by ethereal spirits. A swamper patrol consists of 1d6+6 men-at-arms in leather armor with spears and slings led by a 3 HD sergeant.

# Rumors

When adventurers are seeking information or rumors in a settlement or from the lord of a castle, you can roll a random rumor from the table below. Each rumor is either True ("T") or False ("F") and the hex number associated with the rumor is given in brackets.

| Roll | Rumor | Roll | Rumor |
|---|---|---|---|
| 1 | Poro the oracle wants your entrails (F) **Hex 0105** | 11 | A tiny island holds a wondrous library (T) **Hex 1322** |
| 2 | Shadow wine is delicious (T) **Hex 0113** | 12 | The *helm of darkness* lies where two ridges meet in a stone mouth (T) **Hex 1703** |
| 3 | The sea serpent possesses a maiden frozen in crystal (T) **Hex 0122** | 13 | An obolus provides safe passage to the Earthbound Paradise (T) **Hex 2111** |
| 4 | Heruldos will steal your soul (T) **Hex 0301** | 14 | The great tower is a safe haven for souls (F) **Hex 2205** |
| 5 | Gohl is the portal to a higher plane (T) **Hex 0502** | 15 | The skeleton points the way (T) **Hex 2303** |
| 6 | No good comes from meddling with burial mounds (F) **Hex 0609** | 16 | Egygddedrol's stronghold is a passage to the Earthbound Paradise (F) **Hex 2607** |
| 7 | The colosseum is haunted (T) **Hex 0716** | 17 | Black sands mean your doom (T) **Hex 2804** |
| 8 | Avoid kelp forests – they attract predators (T) **Hex 0822** | 18 | A great treasure lies beneath a meteor (T) **Hex 3011** |
| 9 | Beware the crimson dwarves – they're mad (T) **Hex 1305** | 19 | A powerful artifact is located in a ship stuck in sargassum (F) **Hex 3521** |
| 10 | You have nothing to fear from Ingueas (F) **Hex 1102** | 20 | There is safety on the silver road (F) **Hex 3113** |

# Encounter Key

## 0105.

The woods here are especially thick with ferns of a glossy green-black color that cling to one's clothing. The air is oppressively damp here and one breathes only with a bit of effort. Standing out among the white trees is a wooden tower of black, lacquered wood, about 9-ft in diameter and rising 30 feet high. The tower is unique in that the exterior is completely covered in doors. Forty-five doors (3 feet wide, 6-feet tall) line the exterior, and any one of them, when opened, gives access to the tower.

The interior of the tower is, much like the exterior, a collection of doors. There is no apparent means of ascending from the bottom floor of the tower to its highest level. The rafters of the tower are occupied by a pack of large cats with tortoise-shell markings. The cats will hiss at intruders, but will not initiate combat.

The master of this tower is the wizard Poro. The doors of his tower open into a network of corridors and chambers that adjust their positions depending on the time of day or the wizard's emotional state – he knows where to find things, but others must usually take their chances when they open a door. The complex the doors open into is set in place and dwarves will have the distinct impression that it is quite far underground, based on the temperature, moisture and their general impression of the many tons of stone poised over their heads. The complex has five levels and approximately 50 chambers laid out in a haphazard fashion.

Poro is an oracle by trade, who came long ago into the land beyond the Black Water to read its rocks. The tunnels and chambers of his complex are all carved from the living stone and unadorned that Poro might speak with it as he likes. He records his findings on slates, carving with a diamond-tipped utensil that fits over his right pointer finger and decipherable only with a *read magic* spell. Poro has four apprentices drawn from the embalmer culture. Three are aged 12 to 15 and have attained the first level of magical competence, while the fourth, Gorovan, is 19 and a 2nd level magic-user.

Poro's hideaway is guarded by an earth spirit that looks, at first glance, like a glittering black pudding. In fact, it is formed of black silicates. The creature draws the moisture from those it touches. A fine mimic, it can shape itself into a mirror image of those it encounters, retaining the look of black sand but taking on the form and shape of its subject. It appears to dwell within the earth itself, sliding silently from cracks floor, walls or ceiling. The creature seems to be able to read minds, and it will know if people are intruders or guests of Poro.

Poro's treasure consists of 2,720 gp and a jasper worth 75 gp. It is kept in a brass urn engraved with images of comets.

**Silicate Ooze: HD 12; AC 3 [16]; Atk 1 strike (1d6 plus desiccation); Move 9; Save 3; CL/XP 13/2300; Special: Desiccation (lose 1d3 constitution; one point of constitution is regained by drinking a gallon of water), slowed (as the spell) by water, mimic form.**

**Gorovan, Magic-User Lvl 2: HP 5; AC 9 [10]; Save 14 (12 vs. spells); CL/XP 1/15; Special: Spells (1st). White robe, white headband, dagger, spellbook. Swarthy skinned, black hair, brooding eyes. Facial tic appears when challenged.**

**Master Poro, Magic-User Lvl 9: HP 19; AC 8 [11]; Save 7 (5 vs. spells); CL/XP 10/1400; Special: Spells (5th). White robe, white headband embroidered with gold (15 gp), dagger, spellbook. Pleasant little chap, round face, large eyes, few remaining hairs plastered over his balding head, quick to jest and remarkably graceful for his rotundity.**

## 0109.

The ground at the center of this hex is as black as shadow. Easily avoided in the dayime, the shadowy ground is impossible to see at night. The shadowy ground is insubstantial, and stepping on it will send one falling into a benighted cavern below (30-ft fall).

The cavern is oval in shape and contains a never-ending chariot race. In the center of the arena there is a raised platform of basalt, 10 feet tall and home to a mummy priest called Veporth. Veporth was a priest among the embalmers, but not resides of an eternal race between two charioteers. The first is a shadow with shadow horses, the second a being of flame with horses of fire. The charioteers are fated to race for eternity in a dead heat. When one charioteer gets more than a length ahead of his rival, it is written that the end will come (the Referee can do with this what he or she likes). People falling into the arena will have but a few rounds to clamber to "safety" on the platform, for the charioteers have no compunction about running obstacles down.

Veporth is a priest of Ingueas with the ability to cast spells as a 6th level cleric. He sits enthroned on a seat of gold, his hollow eyes following the racers as they move across his field of vision, but otherwise not moving a muscle. Six canopic jars surround the throne, each holding the undead, disembodied brain of an acolyte. The acolytes can communicate with the Veporth and each is capable of seizing control of a visitor (per the spell *charm person*). Three of the six are aligned with the fire charioteer and three are aligned with the shadow charioteer. They will try to control visitors and set them against the rival charioteer.

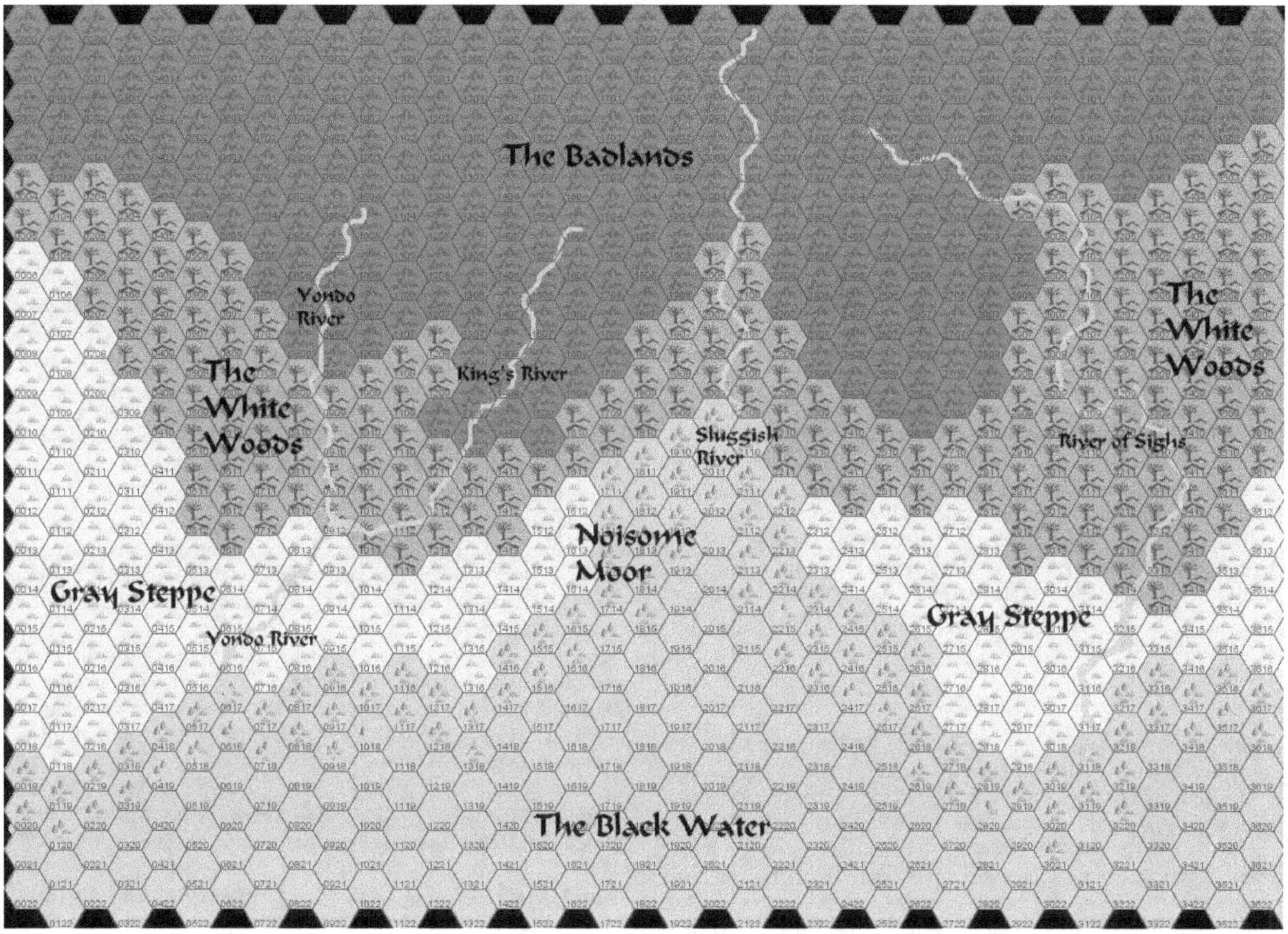

Veporth is wrapped in pristine, white bandages. A golden pyramid floats above his head. The pyramid creates a permanent *shield* effect for the mummy and is also capable of firing rays of darkness and teleporting others. Each hit by a ray cuts the target's strength in half for 1 hour unless they pass a saving throw. Veporth is really more of a philosopher than a threat. He has no treasure other than his throne (worth 250 gp) and the golden pyramid above his head, which operates only for chaotic clerics of 6th level or higher. There is no way to escape the mummy priest's arena other than by teleportation. The mummy priest will provide such a service, but he will require a service in return.

**Shadow Charioteer:** HD 4 (25 hp); AC 4 [15]; Atk 1 whip (1d6 + 1d6 cold); Move 12; Save 13; CL/XP 5/240; Special: Immunity to cold.

**Shadow Horses:** HD 3; AC 7 [12]; Atk 2 hoofs (1d6 + 1d4 cold), bite (1d4 + 1d4 cold); Move 18; Save 14; CL/XP 4/120; Special: Immunity to cold.

**Fire Charioteer:** HD 4 (25 hp); AC 4 [15]; Atk 1 whip (1d6 + 1d6 fire); Move 12; Save 13; CL/XP 5/240; Special: Immunity to fire.

**Fire Horses:** HD 3; AC 7 [12]; Atk 2 hoofs (1d6 + 1d4 fire), bite (1d4 + 1d4 fire); Move 18; Save 14; CL/XP 4/120; Special: Immunity to fire.

**Veporth, Mummy Priest:** HD 6+4 (42 hp); AC 3 [16]; Atk 1 fist (1d12); Move 6; Save 11; CL/XP 7/600; Special: Rot, hit only by magic weapons, *shield*, ray of weakness, teleportation ray, cast spells as 6th level cleric.

## 0113.

A small village of stone huts hidden in a copse of black willows is home to a population of 60 mongrelmen. The leader of the mongrelmen is called Ibler, and has a face that is half troglodyte and half bugbear, a crabman arm and the legs of an ogre and troll. Ibler is a skilled scout and thief. Other prominent citizens of the village include Rennoc the leather-worker and Bibbi, the distiller of shadows. Bibbi has the face of an elf on the torso of a troll with a stunted goblin arm and leg on one side and the arm and leg of a sahuagin on the other.

Bibbi owns several unique implements that allow her to make what the mongrelmen call "shadow wine". Her silver tuning fork makes no sound, but when struck against stone and pointed at an incorporeal spirit it holds them (per the *hold monster* spell). She also owns a silver tube, about 3 feet long and hollow to which she affixes a bottle. The tube can be inserted into the substance of a shadow and drains its essence into the bottle as a thin liquid – the shadow wine. This destroys the shadow. The wine is quite intoxicating, and it fills one's head with mad visions from the shadow's life, imparting to them one skill of the shadow from its life (roll 1d10: 1-5 it is a mundane skill like smithing or fishing; 6-8 it is skill at arms, giving the drinker a +2 bonus to hit; 9 it is the ability to cast spells as a 1d4 level magic-user; 10 it is the ability to cast spells as a 1d2+1 level cleric). The skills last for one hour.

## 0116.

The steppe here is interrupted by a large sand pit. The sand pit is inhabited by large, flat beetles; people who step into the pit will be set upon by 2d4 of the vermin. The bite of the beetles carries painful venom that paralyzes a victim for 1d6 rounds unless they pass a saving throw. The sand pit is similar to quick sand; stepping into it, one sinks about 1d3 feet per round (saving throw each round reduces this to 1 foot of sinking). If the person sinks completely they will lose one level and a new beetle will be born. The person will awake on the shores of the Black Water in a randomly chosen hex. A Referee can put multiple victims in the same or different hexes, depending on how much trouble they want to cause for themselves and their players.

**Sand Beetle: HD 1d3; AC 7 [12]; Atk 1 bite (1d2 plus paralysis); Move 9; Save 18 (16 vs. clerical magic); CL/XP B/10; Special: Paralysis poison.**

## 0122.

Maedain, a wicked old sea serpent that is long and striped blue and black, with multi-faceted eyes and oversized teeth that jut from the sides of its mouth dwells in a dank sea cave decorated with its loot and several figureheads from the black arks of the beyonders. The centerpiece of his treasure is a crystal cabinet containing a woman, apparently frozen in time in mid-scream. The shade of her lover, a powerful wizard, is said to wander hex 0121 calling her name, Felizzon. The remainder of the beast's horde consists of 1,500 sp, 6,370 gp, a cymophane worth 60 gp and a sealed amphora containing 15 pounds of maple sugar (worth 1,000 gp). The wizard's shade knows the following spells that it is willing to teach anyone who rescues his lady love: *extension II*, *hallucinatory terrain* and *rope trick*.

**Sea Serpent: HD 30 (135 hp); AC 2 [17]; Atk Bite (4d10); Move 0 (S18); Save 3; CL/XP 30/8400; Special: Swallow whole.**

## 0202.

An ogre mage dwells in an ornate tower of ivory and bronze in this hex. The tower is shaped vaguely like an arm and fist bursting out of the landscape and reaching toward the heavens. The ogre mage's servants are a band of eight bugaboos, strange creatures that look like decapitated black bears with large bronze spheres, not unlike carved jack-o-lanterns, for heads. The bugaboos are intelligent and crafty, and their eyes burns with fervid malevolence.

The interior of the large tower is divided into four floors, with the fist at the top being the ogre mage's personal chamber of torture. The other floors are each divided into four identical chambers by parchment panels painted in scenes of human misery and defeat in morose watercolors. Each of these chambers holds three bronze lion sculptures with a white smoke drifting out of its mouth, a low, round table holding a red candle and a porcelain tea set (worth 50 gp each) and mats for seating.

The lion sculptures are trapped to belch out an ethereal flame in a 15-ft long cone that is 10 feet wide at the base. The flame inflicts no damage on material objects, but freezes a person's soul for 1d4 points of constitution damage. A person reduced to 0 points of constitution has their spirit burst from their body in the form of a shadow. Lost constitution returns at the rate of 1 point per day.

Each of the aforementioned candles holds the souls of three maidens. When lit, the maidens appear around the table as ghosts. As the candle burns down, the maidens age, finally expiring and free to flee to the earthbound paradise. While in ghost form, the maidens can answer all manner of questions (per the spell *legend lore*), with each maiden offering one answer to one person each time the candle is lit (but no more than one answer per hour). The candles burn out after eight hours of use (roll 1d8 to determine how many hours any given candle has left).

The ogre mage retains a veneer of civilization, and will not kill intruders instantly (well, not all of them). He desires greatly the shadow distiller of the mongrelmen [0113], and may make a bargain to obtain it. The ogre mage's treasure consists of 1,770 sp, 640 gp and a moss agate worth 100 gp.

**Bugaboo: HD 6+1; AC 4 [15]; Atk 2 claws (1d6); Move 15; Save 11; CL/XP 7/600; Special: Fearsome, static shock.**

**Ogre Mage: HD 5+4 (40 hp); AC 4 [15]; Atk 1 tetsubō (1d12); Move 12 (F18); Save 12; CL/XP 7/600; Special: Magic use (*fly*, *invisible* (self), *darkness 10-ft radius*, change into human form, *sleep* 1/day, *charm person* 1/day, *cone of frost* (60-ft long x 30-ft base, 8d6 damage)).**

## 0210.

As you enter this hex, you'll see a gathering of conical gray hills on the horizon. In total, there are five hills, the largest 40 feet tall, the others ranging from 20 to 30 feet in height. The hills have been erected by giant ants with glossy, black carapaces. The ants have a massive network of tunnels beneath the earth – miles of corridors and dozens of chambers, the deepest belonging to the queen. The soil in this hex contains a fair amount of silver, nuggets of the stuff sometimes appearing on the slopes of the anthills, along with strange, purple globules of a waxy, resinous substance. These nodules are to be found deep underground throughout the lands beyond the Black Water. They consist of the solidified memories of departed souls – terribly sad, heavy memories that sink dozens to hundreds of feet into the ground before coagulating with rare earths and forming nodules. Most necromancers have heard of these strange /tones, and prying the secrets and memories out of them is an obsession for some.

**Giant Ant (Worker): HD 2; AC 3 [16]; Atk Bite (1d6 + poison); Move 18; Save 16; CL/XP 2/30; Special: None.**

**Giant Ant (Soldier): HD 3; AC 3 [16]; Atk Bite (1d6 + poison); Move 18; Save 14; CL/XP 3/60; Special: None.**

**Giant Ant (Queen): HD 10 (55 hp); AC 3 [16]; Atk Bite (1d6); Move 3; Save 5; CL/XP 8/800; Special: None.**

## 0218.

This hex contains a field of flatulent geysers that erupt randomly, sending plumes of acidic mist into the air. Breathing is difficult near the geysers, and those unlucky enough to witness an eruption (1 in

6 chance per hour) must pass a saving throw or have their lungs and throat singed, suffering 1d6 points of acid damage and losing the ability to speak or run vigorously for the remainder of the day. The pools of heated water inside these geysers are home to a species of bloated, black sea stars. The creatures, though unthinking, are powerful psychics who pick up the thoughts of those within 200 feet and project images of their loved ones above themselves, as though the person is wading in the water. The images can be interacted with, but they will behave the way the psyched person thinks they should behave, and each person in the area will see different loved ones. The flesh of the starfish is poisonous if consumed, but the dried husks can be burned to produce an acrid smoke that charms intelligent undead (per the *charm monster* spell).

## 0301.

Nestled in a high mountain pass thronged by chattering black mandrills and embraced by thick, chilly mists, is the stronghold of Heruldos, the petty death of murder victims and patron of assassins and poisoners. The stronghold is a modest castle of blue-gray stone and tall, gothic conical towers that disappear into the clouds. A narrow path of crushed onyx leads up the pass to the entrance to the castle, which effectively blocks movement through the pass.

The castle's gatehouse has a tall, thin door of rusty iron that is, in fact, an iron golem disguised by a powerful *phantasmal force*. The gatehouse is guarded by a marilith demon called Lhetoh, who stands atop the battlements shouting challenges at those below, mocking them and goading them to rush the iron door. Like most of the strongholds of the egotistical petty deaths, the castle is really just a grand throne room surrounded by a collection of dusty chambers that seem to exist solely to confuse and frustrate explorers – the deaths and their retinues need neither food nor drink and so have no need for kitchens or pantries, and their existence in this dimensional nexus is tenuous enough that sleep and comfort are generally unneeded. The deaths have control over their strongholds to the point that a room can be what a death desires it to be as needed.

The throne room of Heruldos takes the form of a long torture chamber with a high, vaulted ceiling. Arrow-slits in the upper walls permit the mists and chill of the high mountains to filter into the hall and cause moisture to collect on the walls. A myriad of wheels, screws, racks, bronze cages and iron maidens, braziers steeping red hot pokers and other implements of pain and misery fill the room and are invariably occupied by writhing souls, corporeal and incorporeal. 2d10 dretches shuffle about the chamber, seeing to the prisoner's agony and extracting from them a thin, oily liquid, smoky gray with motes of brilliant emerald and ruby, filling glass tubes capped with lead stoppers. These bottles hold the essence of agony and form the principal fuel for Heruldos and his minions. Mortals that imbibe this liquid gain the abilities of an assassin of equal level for 1 month (or, if already assassins, they gain the abilities of an assassin 3 levels higher) and then find themselves drowning in crushing despair, losing 1d8 points of charisma permanently and another 1d8 points of charisma that return at the rate of 1 point per day. Characters brought to 0 or fewer charisma points by this concoction become misty shades that hide in the corners of Heruldos' castle for eternity.

Heruldos takes the form of a cat-headed man, tall and languid and clad in bone armor made from the remains of his younger sister (who didn't so much defy him as walk by him one day when he felt like killing something). He is cheerful and cunning and without a drop of mercy, though his sloth keeps him from being terribly dangerous. Heruldos is surrounded by a poisonous mist and has the abilities of a 12th level assassin and 9th level magic-user. He can use the following magical abilities: *Fear, invisibility* (self), *mirror image, phantasmal force* and *silence* (centered on anything in his line of sight).

**Heruldos: HD 15 (75 hp); AC -3 [22]; Atk 1 sword (2d6); Move 18; Save 3; CL/XP 22/5000; Special: +1 or better weapon to hit, immune to cold, sees perfectly in any form of darkness, surprises on a roll of 1-9 on 1d10, assassin and magic-user abilities, magical abilities, surrounded by 10-ft radius poison mist (save or die).**

**Lhetoh the Marilith: HD 8 (36 hp); AC -3 [22]; Atk 6 weapons (1d8), tail (1d8); Move 12; Save 8; CL/XP 13/2300; Special: Magic resistance (80%), +1 or better weapon to hit, demonic magical powers.**

## 0321.

A beached narwhale, just barely alive (3 hp) lies here, struggling to breath. The animal swallowed a golden bracelet bearing the arms of a prince of the northern men (first introduced in *Hexcrawl Chronicles #1: Valley of the Hawks*). The prince and his court were escaping from their war-torn country by ship and were lost at sea. One of his siblings would gladly pay for this proof of his death.

## 0408.

Buried beneath the mountains and only accessible after traversing a mile of twisting caverns inhabited by troglodytes, minotaurs and variegated oozes, there is a hidden vault. The vault measures 20 feet wide, 15 feet long and 13 feet tall, with a peaked, arched ceiling. The vault is clad in black marble, cut and placed by expert hands. Twelve pedestals, also of black marble and standing about 4 feet tall, line the walls of the room. In the center of the room there is a statue of a headless woman carved from alabaster with a *robe of many colors* thrown over its shoulders.

On each pedestal there rests a perfectly preserved human head. All of the heads are those of beautiful women, no to quite alike, but all seemingly related. Around each of the head's necks there is a silver gorget set with three fire opals. The fire opals glow with a pale, flickering red light, which becomes fiercer when near a living body. These opals draw energy from the ether or from living bodies to preserve the heads. The heads once belonged to twelve beautiful sisters, the daughters of a archmage. When the archmage was deposed, his body was torn apart and his daughters beheaded. The surviving apprentices of the wizard, some quite powerful mages in their own right, used the silver gorgets (which had been designed by the wizard before his death) to preserve the heads. The alabaster body was carved that it might be animated by the heads. Originally, it was planned that a separate body should be created for each sister, but only one was completed.

The sisters shared the body, contentiously, of course, and forged a powerful kingdom in the land beyond the Black Water, before being again deposed by a union of the petty deaths, who they foolishly sought to eclipse. Should a head be set again on the body, it will animate as a living statue. Each of the sisters has the abilities of a 6th level magic-user, though their grimoires have been stolen and they might only have 1d4 spells prepared when they animate the statue.

**Alabaster Princess: HD 6; AC 4 [15]; Atk 1 slam (1d6+2); Move 9; Save 11; CL/XP 9/1100; Special: Immune to poison and disease, immune to damage from piercing weapons, resistance to damage from edged weapons (50%), resistance to cold, lightning and fire (50%), spells as a 6th level magic-user.**

## 0414.

A village of 20 beehive-shaped stone hovels interrupts the steppe here, surrounded by a tangled thicket and seemingly empty of habitation. The village is inhabited by 45 ghuls, who dwell in burrows beneath the hovels, which they decorate with wind chimes made of bone and dried sinew. The ghuls have no leader *per se*, but rather organize themselves along a "big man" system, following whoever seems to make the most sense at any given time. The ghuls are accomplished, though rather slow, carvers of bone, trading their handiwork to the gnolls for zombies upon which to feast in strange ritual hunts on the steppe. The ghuls possess 220 sp, 795 gp, a tarnished bronze icon of a saint (3 gp), a copper pendant bearing an eldritch sign (300 gp).

**Ghul Warrior: HD 1; AC 7 [12]; Atk 1 weapon (1d6) or strike**

(1d3 plus stun); Move 12; Save 17; CL/XP 2/30; Special: Touch stuns (save negates) for 1d3 rounds.

## 0502.

Gohl, one of the nine petty deaths, dwells in this hex behind a tall copper door placed in the side of a great ridge. The door is guarded inside and out by two lion-headed cherubim encased in armor of black, steel bands and grasping large falchions. Beyond the door there is a long tunnel, well lit by hanging lanterns of every color under the sun – and quite shocking in a land of twilight. The tunnel extends for at least a mile, ending a second door, similarly guarded. Between the great doors are a number of tunnels, each closed by an iron gate (always locked, difficult to pick). These minor tunnels lead to a variety of chambers, all uniformly large with tall, vaulted ceilings that are also illuminated with glass lanters.

Some of these chambers hold dozens of ghostly scribes and philosophers (the souls claimed by Gohl) chained to desks and scratching out scroll after scroll, recording every bit of wisdom they have ever learned (and a few bits they imagine that once learned). The scrolls are collected by pudgy imps dressed in baggy trousers and fez and stowed in niches that line the walls. Almost any question can be answered by these scrolls, assuming one has enough time to sort through the unorganized knowledge and pays the imps enough to fetch the correct scroll.

Other chambers are filled with the mouldering remains of spent sages, bony fingers still wrapped around quills, imps in leather aprons blowing glass globes or making parchment from skins of uncertain provenance, wild eyed dreamers chained to walls and calling out their visions to any who will listen and groups of philosophers working feverishly at solving the riddles of Gohl. Each soul claimed by Gohl must answer a dozen of his riddles before he will usher them on to a higher plane.

Most days (or is it nights – hard to tell in a land of eternal twilight) a steady stream of souls is ushered through the tunnel and past the high throne of Master Gohl, the psychopomp, traveler between worlds. Gohl takes the form of an elderly man of athletic build, unclothed and carrying a human head nestled in the crook of his arm. The head always resembles the person to whom Gohl speaks, and in fact he speaks through the head. Gohl can also take the form of a shadow, and it is in this form that he travels between worlds. In shadow form, his merest touch means death (save at -2 permitted to instead fall into a deep slumber for 1d6 days). Gohl rarely speaks, save to learn what a petitioner wants, what they know, and what they are willing to do to obtain their desire. Gohl can cast spells as a 12th level cleric and 12th level magic-user and can speak all languages and know the alignment of any who meet his gaze.

**Gohl: HD 17 (70 hp); AC -1 [20]; Atk 1 touch (death or slumber); Move 21 (F30); Save 3; CL/XP 24/5600; Special: +1 or better weapon to hit, resistance to cold, fire and lightning (50%), take shadow form, death touch (only in shadow form), magical abilities.**

## 0505.

You enter a long canyon that grows deeper as one travels further into the mountains. The canyon is filled with a petrified forest. About 1 in 100 trees contains a door. The doors cannot be opened from the outside. Knocking on a door brings forth an emerald eye that appears outside the door and floating about 5 feet above the ground. The eye will regard the knocker and, if they are found worthy (roll 1d20 under the knocker's charisma), it opens.

The doors open into a trans-dimensional palace of blinding white light and shadowy pillars placed much as the trees are placed in the surrounding forest. Shadows flit between the pillars, carrying messages back and forth between the planes. Living creatures entering a shadow pillar lose one level and find themselves in some random location, plane or dimension (per the desires of the Referee). Every hour one spends wandering this weird place carries with it two possibilities. The first is a 1 in 6 chance that they will be converged upon by 1d3+1 shadows who will attempt to carry them away into one of the aforementioned pillars. The other possibility is a 1 in 20 chance of meeting Palocar, the master of this place. Palocar is a shadowy figure who seems to grow taller as one grows closer. He coordinates the movements of the shadow demons and has an intimate knowledge of the thousands of portals in the place. Palocar is not malevolent, but it is unfriendly and inhuman and regards people as tools and implements. It might aid travelers if it can discern some gain for itself.

**Shadow: HD 3+3; AC 7 [12]; Atk 1 touch (1d4+strength drain); Move 12 (F15); Save 14; CL/XP 4/120; Special: Drain 1 point of strength with hit, +1 or better weapon to hit.**

**The Palocar: HD 11 (36 hp); AC 2 [17]; Atk 1 touch (1d6+strength drain); Move 15 (F18); Save 4; CL/XP 12/2000; Special: Drain 1d4 points of strength with hit, +1 or better weapon to hit.)**

## 0512.

A herd of spindly centaurs with long faces, obsidian skin and spiked, blue manes ranges over the lake lands here, mostly sticking to the banks of the sluggish, morose river. The centaurs are encountered in groups of 1d6+6 on a roll of 1-3 on 1d6, or 1-5 on 1d6 if one is near the river. They are usually running down an antelope or walking cadaver. The centaurs hunt with bronzewood longbows and carry curved swords. Their leader is Pasco, who has the ability to summon up a variety of spells by speaking riddles while launching his bow. Three times per day he can cast *magic missile* with his longbow, two times per day he can cast *web* with his longbow and once per day he can launch a 5 dice *lightning bolt* with his bow. The centaurs shun treasure, stomping it into the ground or tossing it in the river. They eat their meat raw, and though they don't treat cadavers this way, they still cannot resist running down a walking corpse or scurrying shadow for the sport of it.

**Centaur: HD 4; AC 5 [14]; Atk 2 kicks (1d6), weapon (1d8); Move 18; Save 13; CL/XP 4/120; Special: None.**

**Pasco: HD 5 (33 hp hp); AC 5 [14]; Atk 2 kicks (1d6+1), weapon (1d8+1); Move 18; Save 12; CL/XP 6/400; Special: Spells (*magic missile, web, lightning bolt*)**

## 0520.

The skeleton of a marilith demon juts uncomfortably from a slab of granite, as though a teleportation went awry. Should one manage to free the skeleton, they will discover that two of its hands, now embedded in the slab, carry two curved blades of a black, grainy metal that, though dull in appearance, is remarkably sharp (+1 to hit and damage). These swords, made of zenith metal, are capable of striking incorporeal creatures and absorbing their essence (i.e. save or drained of one Hit Dice or level). When struck together, the blades create a vibration that repels incorporeal creatures for 1d6 rounds. After being freed from the stone, the skeleton will begin to regenerate, with thin membranes and layers of muscle spreading over them in the manner of a film of melting ice being run backwards. In one turn the creature, Skardrra by name, will be complete, though at half normal hit points, and ready to retrieve her blades.

**Skarddra the Marilith: HD 8 (46 hp); AC -3 [22]; Atk 6 weapons (1d8), tail (1d8); Move 12; Save 8; CL/XP 13/2300; Special: Magic resistance (80%), +1 or better weapon to hit, demonic magical powers.**

## 0609.

In the middle of the woodlands there is a large, man-made mound of soil and granite blocks. Broad steps lead up to the top of the mound. Resting on the mound is a rectangular building – 10 feet tall, 12 feet wide and 30 feet long. The buildings are studded with rows of bronze doors, each one locked and giving entrance to a small crawlspace that contains a cadaver. Each cadaver has been dyed a bright color; red, blue, yellow or green. Once a door is opened, the cadaver animates as a 2 HD zombie and attempts to escape its ritual imprisonment. Two or zombies of the same color can merge to become a giant zombie (combine HD, increase AC by one). Up to seven zombies can so merge, with two becoming the size of an ogre (4 HD), three a hill giant (6 HD), four a stone giant (8 HD), five a frost giant (10 HD), six a cloud giant (12 HD) and seven a storm giant (14 HD). In this form, the cadavers have an excellent chance of making it to the Earthbound Paradise, where they can un-merge and dwell in that peaceful land of natural splendor for eternity. There are 28 corpses in all, seven of each color. Cadavers of red and blue attack one another over other targets, likewise with yellow versus green zombies. Should one attempt to communicate with the zombies, they will discover that their minds work in reverse and communication with them (even if they have been destroyed and one *speaks with dead*) leads to confusion (as the spell) unless one passes a saving throw. Inside each of the crawlspaces there is a small sphere of gold held inside a black walnut that has been sealed with gray wax.

## 0612.

A flock of 1d4+4 gaunt night demons perch on a ridge here, watching over the canyons below and snatching up travelers. Those unfortunates who are grabbed are carried into the gray clouds above and dropped to the earth. Their livers are then stolen from the broken bodies by the demons and devoured.

**Night Demon:** HD 4; AC 5 [14]; Atk 1 clutch (1d4); Move 9 (Fly 24); Save 13; CL/XP 8/800; Special: Fear aura, slow motion, +1 or better weapon to hit, immunity to cold.

## 0713.

You come across a lonely figure garbed in rust red armor, head slung low and shield and lance held limply in its hands. The figure rides a brilliant white charger that will snort at the approach of travelers, rousing the rider from its reverie. The Rust Red Knight has been wandering the lands beyond the Black Water for many years, attempting to atone for unspecified behavior that was, he will assure you, quite unforgiving for a knight. The Rust Red Knight – he will give no other name – is of the northern race, with light brown skin, silvery white hair and black, pinpoint eyes. Although generally morose and unresponsive unless roused to do battle, he will leer at beautiful women and, if in their company for more than a day, prove quite a lecher. The Rust Red knight's atonement will be complete when, through clash of arms, his armor has been scraped of rust and once against gleams.

**Rust Red Knight, Fallen Paladin Lvl 8:** HP 47; AC 2 [17]; Move 9; Save 7; CL/XP 8/800; Special: None.

## 0716.

Your travel across the steppe is interrupted by the presence of a ruined colosseum. The origin of the great structure is a mystery. It is constructed of plain, yellowish stones, stacked almost like a child's building blocks with no ornamentation. The structure looks like it can see about 10,000 people and there are three large "boxes" for luminaries, the central box being set higher than the other two. No furniture persists in the strange arena, though a band of 12 ghouls lurks in the tunnels beneath the collosseum, cracking the bones of the large, horrific looking animal skeletons that litter the cages beneath the arena floor. The arena floor is covered in patches of gray witherweed, the woody tendrils of the plants reaching up the walls and into the stands and boxes. The tendrils that cover the central box have also overgrown an alabaster box, about 1.5-feet high, long and wide.

Inside the box, assuming one manages to reach it, are the disembodied souls of 10,000 screaming fans, two parties of noble wraiths (six in all) in yellow togas, with ghostly slaves fanning them

using peacock feathers, and the imperial party in the central box. The imperial party consists of a crypt thing in imperial purple, a thick golden crown on its head, and for feminine spectres in orchid silk gowns embroidered with golden flowers, also fanned by ghostly servants.

The crypt thing will teleport the adventurers into the arena, where they will have to contend with the witherweed and three animated elephant skeletons. The skeletons will appear to burrow up from the ground and then charge. If the adventurers survive, the imperial crypt thing will toss them a bag of 300 large platinum coins bearing his image. Femurs taken from the animal skeletons function as *+1 clubs*.

**Witherweed:** HD 5; AC 6 [13]; Atk 5 fronds (1d4 plus slow); Move 0; Save 12; CL/XP 6/400; Special: Death smoke, slow.

**Skeletal Elephant:** HD 11 (49, 46, 41 hp); AC 6 [13]; Atk 2 stomps (1d8), gore (1d8); Move 15; Save 4; CL/XP 11/1700; Special: Undead, half damage from edged weapons.

**Spectral Ladies:** HD 7 (35, 30, 21, 19 hp); AC 2 [17]; Atk 1 spectral touch (1d8 plus level drain); Move 15 (Fly 30); Save 9; CL/XP 9/1100; Special: Drain 2 levels with hit.

**Noble Wraiths:** HD 4 (17, 12, 11, 11, 10, 10 hp); AC 3 [16]; Atk Touch (1d6 plus level drain); Move 9; Save 13; CL/XP 6/400; Special: Drain 1 level with hit.

**Imperial Crypt Thing:** HD 8 (45 hp); AC 2 [17]; Atk 2 claws (1d6); Move 12; Save 8; CL/XP 11/1700; Special: Teleport other, +1 or better weapon to hit, turn as 12 HD monster.

## 0719.

A thick clutch of white towers cluster along an obsidian shore here, their domes gleaming in the eternal twilight. Windows framed by obsidian tiles interrupt the pearly array, their secrets hidden behind thick curtains. The towers are divided by streets of ashen dust, crowded by the beyonders wrapped in their cloaks, their platform sandals making rectangular divots in the dust. The pedestrians carry birch brooms to sweep away their footprints. Birch trees complete (unsuccessfully) with the towers. Thick, black scaled serpents lounge in the boughs, raising a lazy head on occasion to watch the passersby. Other serpents are led by some beyonders on thin leashes, or are draped across their shoulders. The city is surrounded by a sea of blackberry bushes, the berries being used to dye the cloth of the beyonders. The city is called by its citizens Yondo. It has no rulership, the people dividing themselves into families that compete for secrets, for secrets are the main trade of the beyonders, traded to outsiders for gold and jewels. The families own the towers and the fields of rye and poppies that are worked by reaping zombies. The spiritual leaders of the beyonders are clerical hermits that mummify themselves by drinking poison in small amounts over many, many years. These mummies dwell in shrine towers, sitting atop golden settees and attended by younger priests who go unclothed save for a simple kilt and armed with a black mace. Yondo has representatives of all the normal trades, especially sages, and though they will accept gold at triple the normal prices, they will also trade their goods and services for secrets. The city's harbor is thick with black arks.

## 0804.

A great pile of timber blocks this gorge, apparently knocked down and carried here by a flash flood. A small, brackish reservoir now rests behind the makeshift dam, attracting swarms of mosquitoes and making east-west travel almost impossible. Some (2d6) of the mosquitoes are giant-sized. The mosquitoes now serve as prey for a flock of 2d4 gryphs, mutli-legged black birds with long, needle-thin beaks. At the bottom of the pile of timber there is the body of a magic-user, trapped and unable to complete its journey to the Earthbound Paradise. The magic-user has a slim silver wand of sleep (now bent, 4 charges) and a pouch containing a few small jewels (worth about

80 gp in all) and a copper obolus. The gryphs are clever enough that they will wait for people to be climbing over the timber and harried by the mosquitoes before they attack, usually trying to attack from behind and implant their eggs before fleeing.

**Giant Mosquito: HD 1; AC 4 [15]; Atk 1 touch (attach); Move 12 (F21); Save 17; CL/XP 2/30; Special: Drain blood (1d4 hit points per round, sated at 12 hit points).**

**Gryph: HD 2; AC 5 [14]; Atk touch (attach) or beak (1d8); Move 3 (F21); Save 16; CL/XP 5/240; Special: Attach, implant eggs.**

## 0810.

Chunks of ice and freezing, flammable gasses pour out of hole in the ground. Standing within 10 feet of the hole requires one to make a saving throw each round to avoid suffering 1d6 points of freezing damage and another saving throw to avoid suffering 1d6 points of wisdom damage from the fumes. Any open flame within 10 feet of the hole has a 1 in 4 chance per round of causing a flash explosion of the gas, inflicting 3d6 points of damage to all within 20 feet (save for half). Once an explosion has occurred, the gas will be cleared for 1 turn. The hole is about 20 feet deep and 3 feet in diameter, the interior appearing to be composed of glass formed from extreme heat. At the bottom of the hole there is a small, bronze statue of an amphisbaena, about 1 foot in length. One mouth of the little statue slowly seeps the freezing gas, the other the flammable, wisdom-damaging gas. A small button on each head can stop the gas flow.

## 0818.

A granite hillside rising from the surrounding moors is carved with friezes of what appears to be a beyonder coronation. The hill is carved into three terraces, the lowest depicting large numbers of common beyonders and a number of strange creatures that look like a combination of giraffe, elephant and ibex. The middle terrace shows warriors and noblemen mounted on horses. The top terrace shows a king enthroned and surrounded by bowing demons.

## 0822.

The sea floor rises in this hex and the surrounding hexes such that the water is only about 25 feet deep. A thick forest of kelp covers the sea mount. The forest attracts the unwholesome fish of the Black Water, and thus the creatures that prey on them. Encounters with narwhals occur on a roll of 1 on 1d3 and with the sea serpent Maedain [0123] on a roll of 1 on 1d4.

## 0921.

A basalt sea mount juts up above the waves here at low tide. The mountain is run through with dozens of tunnels and caverns that serve as the lair of a coven of three eyes of the deep. The eyes of the deep collect magical lore and magic items. Their servants are five sea vampires, haggard humanoids that appear to be covered with a thin layer of frost. If caught in the moonlight out of water, they turn into ice sculptures, their hearts becoming large garnets worth 300 gp each. The sea vampires are weaker than their land-based kin and are rather stupid to boot. Hidden within their tunnels, the eyes of the deep have the following treasures: *+1 spear, +3 vs elves* (decreases the constitution of all living creatures within 10 feet of the owner, increasing his hit points by one per stolen point of constitution), *+1 throwing hammer of darkness* (creates darkness in 10-ft radius when held aloft, only usable by males), scale mail composed of turquoise crystals with a quartz pectoral (treat as *+1 leather armor*, allows owner to speak to sea animals), a gorget of gleaming steel (can only be worn by chaotics who have killed a fellow humanoid in cold blood, makes their voices sound like deep, rolling thunder and allows them utter a command once per day to one creature, per the suggestion spell) and a *potion of extra healing* (clear with golden swirls, causes blurred vision for 1 hour after drinking).

**Sea Vampire: HD 4; AC 4 [15]; Atk 1 bite (1d6 plus level drain);**

**Move 12; Save 13; CL/XP 8/800; Special: Bite drains one level (save negates), +1 or better weapon to hit, regenerate 5 hp/hour while submerged, amphibious, assume form of shark or sea urchin.**

**Eye of the Deep: HD 10 (48, 47, 37 hp); AC 4 [15]; Atk 2 pincers (2d4), bite (1d6) and eye rays; Move 3 (Swim 9); Save 5; CL/XP 13/2300; Special: Constrict, eye rays, stun cones.**

## 1007.

The river here is unnaturally calm and clear. One can see gauzy spirits moving up and down the river, their vaguely humanoid shapes barely discernible. People looking into the river will see their reflection slowly turn into that of a mouldering corpse that will slowly reach out to them. Unless the person makes a saving throw, they will be compelled to lean forward and accept the touch of the river spirit. The spirit will steal away a small portion of the person's life force (1d6 hit points). For each hit point stolen, the river spirit may impose one geas upon the person, be they restrictions or quests. A person who follows these rules for one month has their hit points restored; each time a rule is broken the hit point is lost permanently.

## 1015.

Standing or striding through this hex is a curious sight, even by the standards of this region. An iron golem in the shape of an elephant carries on its back a tower of thick wood. The wooden tower, 3 stories tall, is an abbey for a band of monks. The monks number 13 in addition to their abbot, and worship the petty death called Lewl. The monks of Lewl must take a vow of silence (which doesn't prevent them from casting their spells – they replace the verbal component of their spells with rapid eye movements) and poverty, casting away all wealth except magic items. The monks cannot even permit precious metals and stones to enter their tower, and they have trained their colossal mount to do its part in stamping out the evils of wealth (i.e. adventurers laden with gold). While the monks dwell in the tower, contemplating their idol of Lewl, their leader, Kazrabus, is often to be found atop the tower, surveying his domain and interpreting the movement of the clouds to tell the future. On the back of the elephant ride a pack of 12 hobgoblins with red faces, cruel, long tusks and white, bushy hair. The hobgoblins wear chainmail and carry black bows and axes. The hobgoblins hunt in the woods for the monks, using rope ladders to ascend and descend.

**Iron Golems: HD 10 (80 hp); AC 3 [16]; Atk Stomp (4d10); Move 6; Save 3; CL/XP 17/3500; Special: Poison gas (from trunk), immune to all weapons +2 or less, slowed by lightning, healed by fire, immune to most magic.**

**Monk, Cleric Lvl 1: HD 1; AC 3 [16]; Atk Weapon (1d8); Move 12; Save 15 (13 vs. paralysis and poison); CL/XP 1/15; Special: None, rebuke undead.**

**Kazrabus, Cleric Lvl 9: HP 44; AC 3 [16]; Move 12; Save 7 (5 vs. paralysis and poison); CL/XP 12/2000; Special: Spells (5th), rebuke undead..**

## 1019.

In this hex you are apt to encounter 2d4+1 giant komodo dragons on the shore, lapping up the black foam and devouring the bodies that wash up there, releasing the spirits as they do. The reptiles have a spark of intelligence, and are apt to pretend they do not see intruders on their grisly repast until those intruders are within striking distance. Each komodo has a large, black pearl in its stomach. The pearl is worth 1d6x100 gp but possessed by the concentrated bad karma of the souls that have passed through the dragon. Those holding such a pearl must pass a saving throw each time they are tempted by one of the seven deadly sins. Each pearl is possessed of a different sin, determined randomly:

| Roll | Deadly Sin |
|------|-----------|
| 1-3 | Gluttony |
| 4-6 | Lust |
| 7-9 | Greed |
| 10-12 | Despair |
| 13-15 | Wrath |
| 16-18 | Vainglory |
| 19-20 | Pride |

Each time the holder succeeds on a saving throw, the pearl becomes a lighter shade. After seven successful saves, the pearl becomes white and exudes a *protection from evil, 10-ft radius* spell.

**Giant Komodo Dragon: HD 3; AC 5 [14]; Atk 1 bite (1d8 plus venom); Move 12; Save 14; CL/XP 3/60; Special: Lethal venom kills in 1d4+2 rounds.**

## 1102.

The stately manse of Ingueas, petty death of priests and funerary rites, stands atop a plateau surrounded by razor-sharp ridges and overgrown with black willows. A winding path runs the circumference of the plateau, finally passing through a marble arch bearing two sculptures of headless maidens holding long, curved swords. Beyond the marble arch there is a path of crushed, pomegranate-colored stone that runs through thick woodland of willows. The path leads to a single-story marble palace (square in shape, approximately 1,000 ft wide and 1,000 ft. long. The palace is opened to the air, really just consisting of a stepped base, a roof and hundreds of pillars, all in white marble. The pillars divide the palace into a number of square-shaped chambers dedicated to the embalmer's art, the storage of funerary vessels, crates of spices and exotic resins and waiting rooms for the souls she collects.

Ingueas is the keeper of funerary laws and rites and the protector of the dead. To her are allotted the souls of people who were improperly buried. She takes the form of an adult woman with the head of a coursing hound. Ingueas wears an elaborately patterned toga and carries scrolls and an ebony writing kit. She is always surrounded by a gaggle of grim, impish clerks who take down the deeds of the souls she collects, re-animating their mortal forms into undead creatures to dole out proper vengeance on the improperly buried person's relations and priests. Ingueas and her clerks are always in motion, passing from chamber to chamber, recording the deeds of the lost souls and then snuffing out their existence when word reaches her (via imps in the form of magpies) they have been revenged.

**Imp: HD 2; AC 2 [17]; Atk 1 sting (1d4+poison); Move 6 (F16); Save 16; CL/XP 6/400; Special: Poison tail, polymorph, regenerate, immune to fire.**

**Ingueas: HD 16 (78 hp); AC -1 [20]; Atk 1 bite (1d8) or spells; Move 30; Save 3; CL/XP 22/5000; Special: Only +1 or better weapon to hit, casts spells as a 12th level cleric and 12th level magic-user, immune to fear and all undead attacks and abilities, command undead as 20th level cleric.**

## 1112.

The White Wood breaks, revealing a vast meadowland of greenish-gray grass (as wholesome as this nightmare land can get) and red poppies. In the center of the meadow there is a large fortress composed of massive stone slabs. The northern wall of the fortress, which is square in foundation, holds a large gate barred by a grate of white wood and usually left open. The fortress has three levels, each level smaller than the one below it and the uppermost level topped by fierce battlements and a massive, golden gong. The meadow appears to be littered with statues of animals and a few humanoids, all seemingly carved in an approximation of life and motion.

The castle is inhabited by 20 living statues called basilim. Each was born of the meadow, for those walking across it are eventually turned to stone, though they may make a saving throw with each step to resist the power. The first failed saving throw turns the person's heart to stone, stripping them of sympathy and emotional attachment, the second failed saving throw actually petrifying them. So they stand on that meadow as statues for many years, until their will to live finally asserts itself over their frozen forms and they become basilim. Animals are not so lucky, explaining the presence of many more animal than humanoid statues. The basilim believe that their great gong causes the will to live to rise in their future kin, and so strike it a resounding blow at sundown each day. The basilim have little to fear from adventurers, and will make no attempt to check their progress across the meadow, though they will resist entry into their fortress. They have a treasure of 1,500 sp, 60 gp and a pair of platinum earrings worth 3,000 gp.

**Basilim: HD 2+2; AC 5 [14]; Atk 2 slams (1d6); Move 9; Save 3; CL/XP 3/60; Special: Madness, half damage from non-magical weapons.**

## 1209.

Atop a wide dais of swirled pink and white marble there is a massive statue of a giant centipede composed of clear crystal. In the middle of the giant centipede there is embedded a silver two-handed sword. The crystal can be shattered with a blow from a bludgeoning weapon that inflicts 9 points of damage. If this occurs, the crystal statue collapses into thirty shards that turn into a giant centipedes. The sword will continue to hand 8 feet above the ground in mid-air until one grasps the handle and declares themselves to be the sword's master. The sword is edged in silver and otherwise acts as a *+1 two-handed sword, +3 vs. vermin*. If the holder of the sword is struck by bright light, he acts as though *feebleminded*.

**Giant Centipede: HD 1d2; AC 9 [10]; Atk Bite (1 + poison); Move 13; Save 18; CL/XP 2/30; Special: Lethal poison (+4 save)**

## 1217.

The skeleton of a colossal frog lies half buried in the muck here. The skeleton is covered in vines. Should one move within the beast's rib cage, the vines will form a cage and the skeleton will arise from the muck, trapping the explorer. The skeleton will begin to hop away in a random direction, carrying the hapless adventurer 1d6 hexes away in a single day. If moving more than 3 hexes in a day, others will be hard pressed to keep up. Once it has reached its destination (which might be under water), the frog skeleton falls apart and releases its victim. The skeleton has an Armor Class of 3 [16] and withstands 8 dice of damage before falling apart. The person inside the ribcage can escape by making a successful open doors roll.

## 1305.

Atop a peak in this hex there is a clan of crimson-skinned dwarfs laboring on a massive tower that uses the mountain as its foundation and has so far been built to a height of 500 feet. The dwarfs are obsessed with the notion of reaching the moon, where, they assure visitors, nuggets of mithral tumble down silvery rivers from the gray mountains. The dwarves are, of course, quite mad. They have hollowed out the upper portions of the mountain quarrying stone for their tower, which now houses 600 dwarves, some of the clans living so far apart as to hardly know the dwarves constructing the portion of the tower opposite their own. The dwarves are ruled by a council of priests who worship the moon (the Silvery Face That Blesses the Heavens, as they put it), wearing large silver talismans stamped with the face of the man in the moon and wearing black robes. The dwarf priests shave their heads (and bodies) of hair, whereas their subjects are not permitted to cut their hair as long as they live. As a result, the dwarves have long beards that they braid and wear wrapped around their bodies and tucked into their belt. This mass of hair (it takes two full days to wash) provides them an additional +1 bonus to AC, but slows them to a movement rate of 3.

Dwarf warriors in the clan wear chainmail and carry round, white shields and crescent axes. Sergeants (3 HD, one per 10 dwarves) and captains (6 HD, one per 5 sergeants) of the dwarves wear platemail and often have weapons edged in silver. The priests number 30 and are all clerics (roll 1d6 for level) in platemail and wielding heavy lead maces traced with silver. The chief of the priests is an elderly man called Clovis. Clovis has a braided beard so long that it is borne behind him by two pages. His teeth are crooked and his eyes are wild with the fervor of his belief.

The crimson dwarves are, as was previously mentioned, mad, and attempts to read their minds or carry on long conversations with them end in *confusion* for 1d6 days unless a saving throw is passed. They are immune to mental affects.

**Crimson Dwarf: HD 1; AC 3 [16]; Atk Weapon (1d8); Move 6; Save 17; CL/XP 1/15; Special: *Confusion* from mind reading, dwarf abilities.**

## 1313.

The warlord Erlike, a fourth-category demon (i.e. nalfeshnee) commands a small army of 120 giant boar mounted orcs wearing blackened chainmail and carrying horseman's axes and bolos (the balls are made of ivory and carved to look like skulls – the orcs are quite proud of this and will take great pains to show them off to victims and discuss the craftsmanship). Erlike looks like an aged man with a wrinkled though muscular body, the face and tusks of a pig with black eyes and bushy, steel-gray eyebrows and a long mustache.

Erlike and his army are camped outside the walls of a town called Cuth. The men of Cuth are worshipers of a large, demonic, scaled lion called Nergal. Cuth is a massive tower keep with walls 80 feet tall built of polished obsidian and sloping out from top to base. Within the structure dwell 580 men, women and children. The stores are almost run out, and their "god" has taken to devouring the old, young and others considered unfit for war. Each day, the men of Cuth ascend to the tops of their walls, sound brass horns and then blacken the skies with their arrows. Many orcs (1,200 in all) have perished from these assaults, but still Erlike waits. When the shower of arrows ends, the orcs use their engines of destruction to hurl great stones at the walls of the keep, to little effect. The treasury of the keep holds a shield made of living black metal. The shield carries a +2 enchantment and has an ego of 13. It is possessed by the spirit of an ancient, cruel king who will attempt to drive the bearer of the shield to greater and greater conquests and slaughters. In addition to its basic enchantment, the shield has the ability to cloud minds (treat as invisibility) once per day and forced non-magical weapons that strike it (i.e. weapon attacks that missed hitting the bearer by 3 or less points) to save or be absorbed into the metal. Each metal weapon so absorbed can be launched as a metal sphere one round later. These spheres have a range of 30 feet and deal damage as the weapon they absorbed.

**Erlike: HD 11 (41 hp); AC -1 [20]; Atk 2 claws (1d4), 1 bite (1d6+2); Move 9 (F14); Save 4; CL/XP 13/2300; Special: +1 or better weapon to hit, magic resistance (65%), +2 on attack rolls, immune to fire, magical abilities.**

**Nergal: HD 9 (65 hp); AC 0 [19]; Atk 2 claws (1d6), bite (2d6+1); Move 18 (F9); Save 6; CL/XP 12/2000; Special: Roar (all who hear must save or suffer -1 penalty to all attacks for 1 turn), cast spells as 10th level cleric.**

## 1322.

A small island – really just an octagonal tower keep poised atop a rocky outcropping – is located in this hex. The island is surrounded by a number of other vicious looking rocks that suggest a stone claws reaching out of the water to grab the fortress and pull into beneath the waves. One enters the fortress through an iron door located roughly 15 feet above the surface of the water. This door is unlocked. The door leads into an outer hallway that runs completely around the fortress (a circuit of about 75 feet, given that the diameter of the fortress is approximately 40 feet and the outer walls are 8 feet thick.

The floors and ceiling of this passage are composed of amber stone, though in one place there are 20 copper rods embedded in the ceiling. Should any one of these be anointed with fresh blood (human or animal), they will descend as a staircase, opening up an entry into the upper gallery of the fortress.

The upper gallery runs around the perimeter of the fortress and looks down on an octagonal library 20 feet in diameter. The eight walls of the library contain wooden shelves piled high with books, papers and scrolls (see sidebar for precise composition). One hundred volumes are present in the room. Accompanying the books and scrolls on the shelves are twelve porcelain dolls, all showing some wear and tear and all staring at the figure in the center of the room with unblinking glass eyes. Above the gallery there is a vaulted ceiling and thick rafters. The domed ceiling/roof of the room, hidden from the outside by the thick amber walls, is composed of thin alabaster, allowing a small measure of light to filter through into the chamber, which is otherwise unlit.

In the center of the room, sitting at a reading desk, is a skeletal figure in a copper-red robes, chin propped on a hand and ghostly green eyes moving back and forth over the page of a dusty, leather tome regarding the mystical formulae to be derived from the migratory patterns of gulls. This scholar is the lich lady Adrimiret. Obsessed with the collection of knowledge from across the world, she will pay little heed to visitors unless they attack her or her books. Her friends (see below) are perhaps overly protective of her, and might attack with little or no provocation.

Adrimiret's friends are the porcelain dolls. The dolls are not animated, but they are possessed by powerful, malevolent spirits called moppes.

**Moppe: HD 1; AC 11 [8]; Atk none; Move 0; Save 17; CL/XP 3/60; Special: Spells.**

**Adrimiret, Lich: HD 12 (52 hp); AC 0 [19]; Atk 1 hand (1d10+paralysis); Move 6; Save 3; CL/XP 15/2900; Special: Appearance causes paralytic fear, touch causes automatic paralysis, spells as 12th level magic-user.**

## Random Knowledger

| Roll | Ephemera |
| --- | --- |
| 1 | Book (5 lb) |
| 2 | Tome (10 lb) |
| 3 | Scroll (3 lb) |
| 4 | Loose Folio (1 lb) |

| Roll | Knowledge |
| --- | --- |
| 1 | History |
| 2 | Geography |
| 3 | Magic (arcana) |
| 4 | Theology (religion) |
| 5 | Cosmology (the planes) |
| 6 | Nature |

## 1401.

The top of a mountain peak here has been carved into a stepped pyramid. Each stage of the pyramid measures 22 feet wide and the next step is seven feet above. In all, there are five steps. On each of the four lower steps there is a long table of marble and benches of golden wood. Atop the table there are cups of fragrant incense and platters heaped high with empty boasts and unrealistic dreams that appear as candied plums to the shades that feast on them. The shades of the pyramid are the property of Lewl, the petty death that claims the souls of nobles and aristocrats.

Lewl himself is enthroned atop the pyramid. Grim as death he sits, quietly watching the antics of the assembled high born shades. Lewl stands 12 feet tall. He has plum-colored eyes, blue skin and a long, pointed nose. His arms and fingers are unnaturally long, and can stretch up to 12 feet when he desires. He mostly uses this power to snatch the unruly shades and inhale their essence into his own. Lewl wears robes that reflect the night sky and he carries a golden scepter.

Despite his fondness for consuming souls, Lewl is well spoken and gentile. He is happy to entertain guests, but will warn them not to partake of the feast, lest they become as vainglorious and useless as his shades. Lewl is quite the gossip about his fellow petty deaths, and is apt to become fond of adventurers with a ready wit and impeccable manners.

**Lewl: HD 12 (65 hp); AC -1 [20]; Atk 1 +1 scepter (1d8+1); Move 12; Save 3; CL/XP 14/2600; Special: Only harmed by +1 or better weapons, immune to fear, stretch arms (10-ft), drain levels or Hit Dice from shades.**

## 1407.

As soon as a party of adventurers enters this hex, they will be stalked by an ancient manticore, its broad face possessed of gray whiskers and gleaming white eyes, some of its teeth broken. The manticore has a lair in this hex, a depression surrounded by ancient, weathered stones covered with alabaster moss. Within the lair are the skulls of its many kills, scattered about rather recklessly. His treasure is kept buried and consists of 2,270 sp and 290 gp. The manticore is exceptionally grumpy, the skulls of its past kills having a tendency to chatter all night long. The talking skulls are a way for a Referee to introduce rumors (or lies) to the players.

**Manticore: HD 6+4 (34 hp); AC 4 [15]; Atk 2 claws (1d3), bite (1d8), 6 tail spikes (1d6); Move 12 (F18); Save 11; CL/XP 8/800; Special: Flight, hurl spikes 180 feet.**

## 1502.

The well worn pages of a spellbook are plastered against damp cliffs that overlook a rushing stream in this hex. If collected, one will find most of the pages damaged beyond recognition. Those that remain readable contain 1d3 level one spells. All of the pages, whether readable or not, will animate if folded into animal shapes and can be used to carry messages or scout ahead. If sent ahead as scouts, they return within the hour and unfold, the sights they saw being written on the paper in a beautiful, flowing script.

## 1515.

Stretching across the wretched plain is a column of slaves driven by whining and cackling gnolls. On closer inspection, one will discover that the slaves are zombies, chained at wrist and ankle, and linked to their fellows by leather collars and tongs. At the head of the column there is a albino gnoll, a shaman, sitting atop a crude wooden palanquin carried by eight zombies. The shaman feeds on delicate, though macabre, morsels with a silver fork, and imp strumming lightly on a miniature mandolin sitting at his feet and intoning weird songs in a surprisingly deep voice. In all, there are 20 gnolls, 100 zombies and the aforementioned shaman. The gnolls have patchy, golden-brown fur, wear crude ring armor and carry black flails and battered wooden shields. One out of every 10 gnolls is an overseer equipped with a barbed whip – the whips do little to motivate the zombies, but they satisfy something particularly dark and savage in the overseers – and a silver dagger. The gnolls are middle men – forming a trade link between the villages of the steppe and the swamp people. They are currently heading east to Hex 2409.

**Zombie: HD 2; AC 8 [11]; Atk Strike (1d8); Move 6; Save 16; CL/XP 2/30; Special: Immune to sleep and charm.**

**Gnoll: HD 2; AC 5 [14]; Atk Bite (2d4) or weapon (1d10); Move 9; Save 16; CL/XP 2/30; Special: None.**

**Gnoll Overseer:** HD 4; AC 5 [14]; Atk Bite (2d4) or whip (1d6 + stun); Move 9; Save 13; CL/XP 4/120; Special: Whip stuns for 1 round (save to negate).

**Grxxx, Gnoll Shaman:** HD 5d6; AC 5 [14]; Atk Bite (1d6); Move 9; Save 12; CL/XP 5/240; Special: Cast spells as 3rd level cleric.

## 1520.

This hex and those around it host an unwholesome coral reef. The reef is based around the remains of a sunken black ark, and a number of beyonder skeletons remain embedded in the reef. The primary inhabitants of the reef, aside from the white, slimy fish of the Black Water, are giant moray eels. Encounters with the 1d6 of the eels occur on a roll of 1-3 on 1d6 each day one spends plumbing the cracks and crevices of the reef. There is the potential (percent chance each day equal to highest wisdom score in the group) of finding 1d4 x 100 gp worth of treasure while exploring the reef.

**Giant Moray Eel:** HD 4; AC 7 [12]; Atk 1 bite (2d6); Move 0 (S9); Save 13; CL/XP 4/120; Special: None.

## 1612.

Travelers through this hex have a 2 in 6 chance per day of encountering a floating death altar. The death altar appears as a construction of onyx stone, a platform 20 feet in diameter topped by a rectangular sacrificial altar that glows with a reddish light. Around the sides of the platform there are set five large bloodstones, each worth 700 gp. These bloodstones emit cones of reddish light (60 feet long, 40 feet wide at base) that cause a person's blood to boil. The cones of light inflict 4d6 points of damage, though a target can make a saving throw to save for half damage. Creatures that suffer more than 15 points of damage from this light gain a permanent reddish tinge to their skin and lose all of their hair. Creatures that suffer more than 25 points of damage from this light permanently lose 1d6 points of wisdom and intelligence (roll separately for each).

Aboard the death altar are fifteen drunken satyrs and a nymph dressed in orange robes covered with silk embroidery that resembles peacock feathers. On the palm of her left hand she has painted a toothy mouth and on the right a bloodshot eye. Touching a creature with the left hand causes damage as per a *cause light wounds* spell. Touching with the right hand forces the person to live out their worst memory, per a *phantasmal killer*. The death priestess can also cast spells as a fourth level cleric. Her satyr followers suffer a -2 penalty to hit from their drunkenness. All of them carry short bows with barbed arrows. A creature that takes maximum damage from such an arrow has it lodged in their armor and flesh. The arrow inflicts 1d4 points of damage when removed, and lowers the armor's bonus to Armor Class by one thereafter. Until the arrow is removed, the afflicted always goes last in combat.

**Satyr:** HD 5; AC 5 [14]; Atk 1 weapon (1d8); Move 18; Save 12; CL/XP 6/400; Special: Magic resistance (50%), concealment.

**Death Nymph:** HD 6 (37 hp); AC 9 [10]; Atk none; Move 12; Save 14; CL/XP 10/1400; Special: Sight causes blindness or death, cast spells as 6th level cleric.

## 1703.

In the upper regions of a place where two razor-sharp regions meet there is a large gash in the side of the mountains, a cave that suggests a gaping maw of rotten teeth. A tiny, black rivulet pours from the "mouth", splashing down the narrow valley and collecting in a number of pools that sparkle with the movement of tiny, silver fish. Beyond the "mouth" there is a cave complex composed of a number of limestone caverns the wind through the interior of the mountains. The ceiling of this cavern is home to a swarm of 20 giant bats. The black rivulet runs through most of the caverns, originating in a hemispherical cavern of rose quartz. The black river originates here, pouring from the mouth of a large, quartz head.

The water causes anything it touches to become permanently insubstantial (per *oil of etherealness*) – a hand might fade into nothingness, invisible and unable to grasp anything in the material world, but the hand's owner can feel it nonetheless. Lodged inside the mouth and partially blocking the flow is the infamous *Helm of Darkness*, an artifact of the land beyond the Black Water sought after by the petty deaths and their followers.

The *Helm of Darkness* can grant *invisibility* to its wearer at will, and gives the wearer the ability to see in *darkness*, see invisible creatures, *speak to dead* and grants them a +2 bonus to save vs. illusions.

Dwelling in the pool is a seven-headed hydra with shining golden scales that, once it emerges from the inky water, fills the cavern with bright light. On the end of its seven necks are cherubic faces that can open their mouths unnaturally wide, bearing serpentine fangs.

**Giant Bats:** HD 4; AC 7 [12]; Atk Bite (1d10); Move 4 (F18); Save 13; CL/XP 5/240; Special: None.

**Celestial Hydra:** HD 7 (40 hp); AC 5 [14]; Atk 7 bites (1d6); Move 9; Save 9; CL/XP 9/1000; Special: Regenerate 2 hp per round, double damage to chaotics.

## 1706.

An ancient royal tomb is hidden in this hex. It can be entered by a narrow cleft in the cliffs overlooking the infant river, a cleft so cleverly hidden by the surrounding undulations of the stone as to be the equivalent of a concealed door. The entry passage zigzags back a ways, eventually reaching a junction containing a secret door (A). The door is opened by putting pressure on the top and pivoting the door just enough to allow one to crawl through.

**B** – This room is the antechamber the false crypt. The antechamber is decorated in yellowish-gray marble and has piles of soot piled in the corners and charred bones in the center. A scorched chain also hangs in the center. On the walls opposite the charred bones and scorched chain there are two deep bas-reliefs of dragons in bronze fastened to the walls, their mouths wide open. The mouths are trapped to breath cones of fire that inflict 6d6 points of damage to anything in the center of the room. The trap is armed as soon as the doors to the false crypt are opened and tripped when something steps on a pressure plate in the center of the room. The chain actually disarms the trap and reveals the secret door behind the one dragon's mouth.

**C** – This false crypt contains a parliament of skulls – 200 in all. The skulls have glass gemstones implanted in them and sealed with wax. When anything enters the crypt, the skull's "eyes" light up and they emit a hissing sound. The gas is highly psychoactive, causing bizarre hallucinations for 1d4 hours. The skulls and their gems are completely worthless.

**D** – One reaches this chamber by crawling through the dragon's mouth. It is a tight fit for anything but a goblin or halfling. The chamber is clad completely in thick tiles of black glass. The glass covers a pool of black water inhabited by a dozen floating eyes. The middle of the room is open to the water. The black glass tiles and black water make this difficult to discern, and folks walking through the river have a 3 in 6 chance of falling into the water (elves and dwarves have only a 2 in 6 chance). A golden talisman hangs on the wall opposite the entrance. The wearer of this amulet must pass a saving throw or imagine plunging through the earth as though insubstantial. In fact, they will begin rolling around on the ground like a fool, increasing their chance to fall into the water to 5 in 6.

**Floating Eye:** HD 1d6; AC 3 [16]; Atk 1 bite (1d2); Move 0 (S24); Save 18; CL/XP 1/15; Special: Hypnotic gaze, surprise on a roll of 1-5 on 1d6.

**E** – This is the true crypt's antechamber. It walls are lined with six empty suits of armor hanging on wooden skeletons. The suits of armor have helms with demon masks. The demon masks have crystal eyes that, if looked into, force a person to don the helm and take up arms against the tomb robbers.

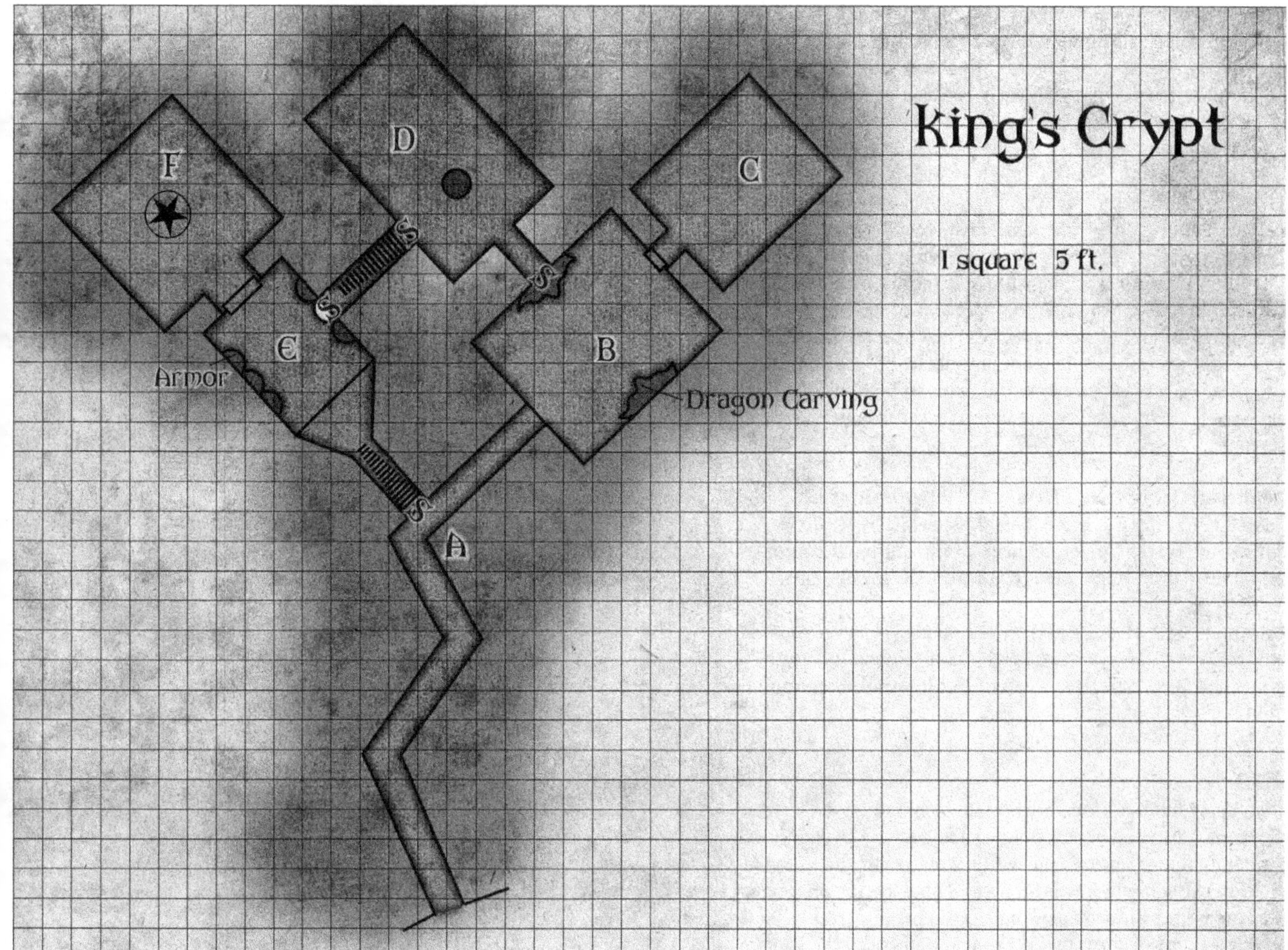


**F** – Behind the bronze door of the crypt there is a pink-orange marble slab carved to look like a coiled dragon. Sitting atop a tall saddle on the dragon's back is the mummified remains of an embalmer king. The king is clad in ceremonial armor of gold scales (worth 300 gp) and holding a razor-sharp pole arm in each arm. The pole arms are actually connected to the dragon. When one steps into the tomb, they trigger a trap. In exactly 3 minutes, the stone dragon and its rider begin to spin rapidly in the center of the room. Anyone near the strange funeral slab must pass a saving throw or suffer 2d6 points of damage from the dragon and glaives. Moreover, the spinning stirs up a thin layer of red tomb dust. Anyone in the chamber must pass a saving throw or breathe the dust into their lungs. The dust is composed of miniscule shards that lacerate the lungs, causing 1 point of constitution damage each day (no save). After half a person's constitution has been lost, they will begin coughing up blood. The dust can only be defeated through the use of a *cure serious wounds* spell and *remove curse* spell cast one directly after the other. The tomb contains two bolts of purple silk (each 50 yards, 6 lb, worth 500 gp), crates of salt bricks (30 pounds, 150 gp), 1,700 sp and 680 gp

flock of pearly white pseudo-dragons that roost atop the tower and flit in and out of the large, round portals that serve as windows. The pseudo-dragons' only weakness is music and song, which forces them to make a saving throw or be entranced. Nakwathaz' treasure, disguised as a vat holding paraffin wax, consists of 4,900 gp, a banded agate worth 45 gp and a terracotta chalice worth 5 gp – it was owned by his mother and is a treasured keepsake.

**Pseudo-Dragons: HD 2; AC 2 [17]; Atk 1 bite (1d3), tail sting (1d3+poison); Move 6 (F25); Save 16; CL/XP 5/240; Special: Poison (catalepsy for 1d4 days), magic resistance (25%).**

**Twin Apprentices, Magic-User Lvl 1: HP 2 each; AC 9 [10]; Move 12; Save 15 (13 vs. spells); CL/XP B/10; Special: Spells (1st). Black tunic, white leather belt, wavy-bladed dagger.**

**Nakwathaz, Magic-User Lvl 10: HP 29; AC 9 [10]; Save 6 (4 vs. spells); CL/XP 11/1700; Special: Spells (5th). Equipment, spellbook.**

## 1711.

A charming tower like an ivory flute rises from the brambles and blackberry bushes that carpet this hex. The tower rises 50 feet and emits a low hum into the countryside, a hum that causes people's sanity to slowly slip away (lose 1 point of wisdom per hour unless a saving throw is made; at 0 wisdom the character is struck with permanent *confusion*). The owner if the tower is the magic-user Nakwathaz, a handsome, well-proportioned man dressed in a leather loincloth and harness. Nakwathaz is above all a trickster, and very skilled with the spell *phantasmal force* (opponents are -2 to save vs. his illusions). Nakwathaz has two apprentices, twins, taken from the swampers. The twins have had their heads shaved and wear black tunics and white, leather belts. Nakwathaz' tower is guarded by a

## 1913.

Across several acres of the murky, chilly swamp there are scattered thirty wattle-and-daub huts atop 10-ft tall stilts. The huts sit on a platform large enough to afford the inhabitants a 3-ft wide ledge. These ledges are cluttered with clay pots and dried gourds containing herbal mixtures. The interior of each hovel is home to 1d4+3 swampers, along with their pets (usually non-venomous serpents, sometimes dull, gray toads). The tribe's giant swine live on dry bits of land in wooden pens and guarded by the old warriors of the tribe, men in coats of tarnished copper rings and carrying spears and slings. All of the swampers are skilled herbalists and about 1 in 6 has the abilities of 1st to 4th level druid.

The unacknowledged leader of the swampers is a tall, elderly woman called Zepheret, with exceptionally long hair woven into dozens of thin braids that cling to her ample frame. Zepheret is a bit senile, but still commands the respect of the others, not least of which because of her ability to summon mud men from the bottom of the swamp. She keeps 400 gp in her hovel sealed inside a dozen dried gourds with wax, as well as 20 pounds of salt (worth 5 gp per pound). The gourds are strung together and hang from the ceiling. Zepheret keeps three vipers in her hovel as guard animals and companions, and they seem to have rubbed off on her, for she has a serpent's cold stare and speaks with a sibilant lisp. Zepheret's latest project is an old, leathery corpse that lies in the middle of her hovel. She has traced hundreds of swirling lines on its skin, covering about 80% of it, using an ink mixed from rare herbs and acids. When finished, she believes her handiwork will animate the corpse as a zombie servant.

**Zepheret, Druid Lvl 7: HP 27; AC 9 [10]; Move 12; Save 9 (7 vs. fire); CL/XP 9/1100; Special: Spells (4th), determine water purity, identify plants, move through undergrowths, shape change, immune to fey charms.**

**Mudmen: HD 2; AC 7 [12]; Atk 2 slams (1d4) or mud bomb; Move 6; Save 16; CL/XP 5/240; Special: Engulf, mud bomb, +1 or better weapon to hit, mindless, mud pool**

## 2004.

Atoda is the petty death who takes charge of those who die from old age or unfortunate accidents. He dwells in a manor of gray brick and white wood with thick-paned windows. Each window is home to a ghostly doppelganger that takes the form of any that look into its window and then arises to destroy them. From the outside, the manor would appear to contain many rooms, but it is in fact one large chamber. Dozens of shades, bent and feeble, shuffle around the chamber under the watchful eyes of Atoda, who sits like a nomadic despot upon a throne of shadows surrounded by a circle of spears thrust into the wooden floor.

Atoda wears a silk deel of gray emblazoned with golden chrysanthemums. In the morning, he appears as a young man, but ages as the day proceeds. In all forms he is short and wide-chested and in place of hair has long spines like those of a sea urchin. He has ruddy skin and large, umber eyes. On his lap he holds a crossbow that fires *magic missiles* (3/day) as though from a 15th level magic-user. Atoda knows the destiny of gods and men, and even shares this information in return for a favor. He can assume the form of a giant tiger at will.

**Atoda: HD 15 (90 hp); AC -2 [21]; Atk crossbow or as tiger (double damage); Move 9; Save 3; CL/XP 20/4400; Special: Only harmed by +1 or better weapons, casts spells as a 6th level magic-user, immune to fear and fire, assume the form of a giant tiger (as tiger but double hit dice and damage) at will.**

## 2009.

A giant, spectral tree rises from the forest here, its branches piercing the gray clouds above. Ghostly rats can be seen crawling up and down the tree (at least 1d8 will attack anyone attempting to climb the tree). The upper portion of the tree grants access to another dimension, an infinite, glassy obsidian plain on which rainbow hued warriors engage in eternal war. There is a 1 in 6 chance that an obsidian axe or dead body will plummet from the clouds, with a small chance of it landing on standing beneath it.

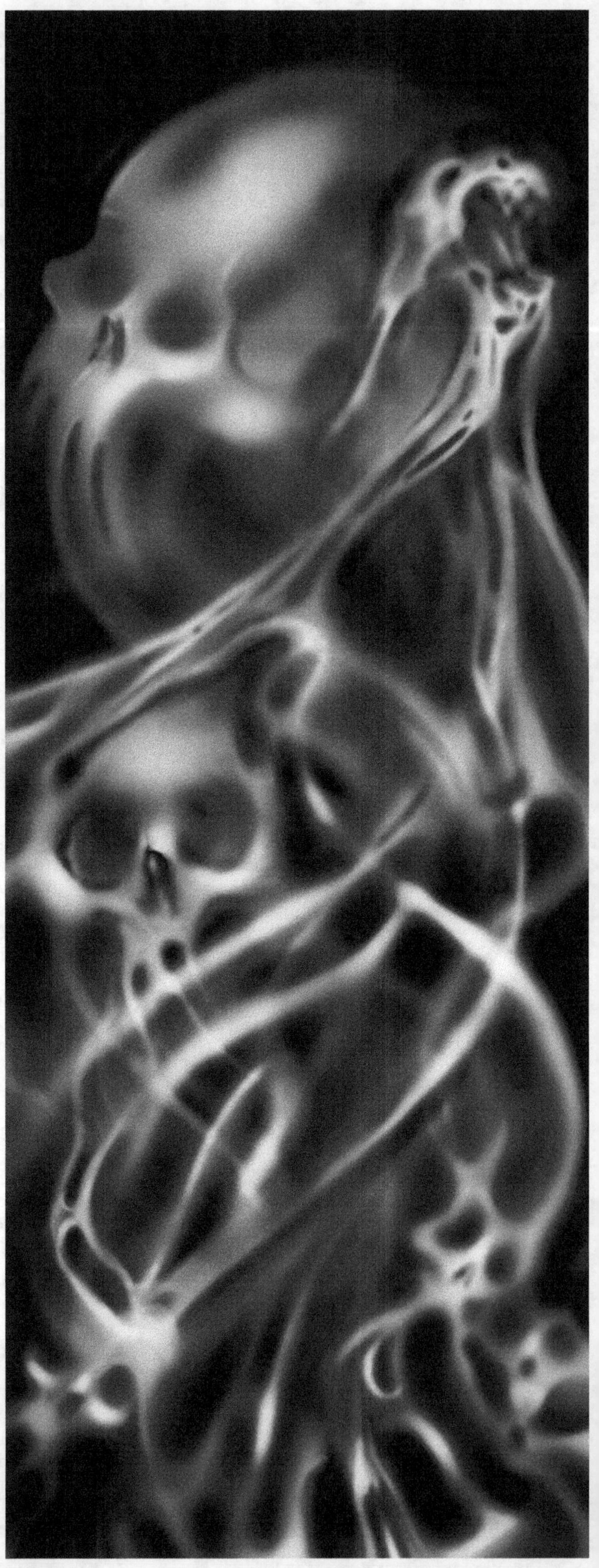

## 2108.

You perceive three boatmen poling a barge of grayish wood up the river. The barge is stacked with what appear to be corpses, stacked like cord wood and held to the barge with chains. Two the boatmen, in simple brown hooded robes, pole the boat, while a third sits atop the grisly mound armed with a crossbow. If one watches long enough, they will perceive the crossbowman launch his missile toward something in the water, often something reaching out of the water and then disappearing as the bolt strikes them with a squishy thud or just splashes into the water near them. The boatmen are wraiths, and there is a 1% chance that a body sought by the adventurers is stacked on their barge.

**Wraith: HD 4; AC 3 [16]; Atk 1 touch (1d6+level drain); Move 9 (F24); Save 13; CL/XP 6/400; Special: Drain 1 level with hit.**

## 2111.

On the banks of the river there is a large, square building of stone blocks with ever-burning chimneys. Inside the hellish building there is a great forge. A clan of dour dwarves, ashen-skinned with wrinkled, hairless faces, work day and night minting copper coins. The copper coins, called obolus, provide safe passage for souls traveling up the river, but they must be purchased with secrets, dark and dangerous secrets. In turn, the dwarves can trade these secrets to the great families of the beyonders, or send them via carrier pigeons to associates across the Black Water to make other uses of them. The clan consists of 20 dwarves, their leader being Groturk, a wizened character with a slightly oversized glass eye that can cast *fear* once per day as a 30-ft cone. Groturk and his clansmen (no women are in evidence) wear thick leather aprons and carry sledge hammers, tongs, chisels and other tools of the minter's trade. A ton of copper nuggets fill the corners (worth about 200 gp). The copper is mined in the north.

**Dwarf: HD 1+1; AC 8 [11]; Atk 1 weapon (1d6+1); Move 6; Save 17 (15 vs. magic and poison); CL/XP 1/15; Special: Dwarf abilities.**

**Groturk: HD 6+6; AC 8 [11]; Atk 1 weapon (1d8+1); Move 6; Save 11 (9 vs. magic and poison); CL/XP 7/600; Special: Dwarf abilities, cause fear with glass eye.**

## 2121.

The black sea churns here, descending into a whirlpool. The whirlpool is actually the maw of a leviathan, a giant whale some 300 feet long. The beast sucks in water for a week, and then expels it for a week. The whirlpool is large enough to suck in a large ship. Once inside the beast, one might find themselves in good company, for the creature's digestion is quite slow and many have fallen prey to it. These castaways now dwell in the beast's digestive system, living off the fish that are sucked into the leviathan.

## 2205.

The winding river ends here in a subterranean harbor ringed by battlements, towers and quays of black stone staffed by shuffling zombies in white tunics and bronze pectorals, their fleshed tattooed with queer symbols. Above the dome of iridescent limestone containing the harbor there is a stout, black tower – a counting house of souls, center of judgment in the land beyond the Black Water. Corporeal souls are herded into dark pits to await judgment, being hauled from their confinement by kytons waiting on ledges above and awaiting instruction via bronze tubes that crisscross the weird fortress. Incorporeal souls enter the place via trade and are usually stored in glass containers which are transported by imps garbed in costumes of satin and lace.

Dwelling in this fortification are the three judges Minos, Rhadamanthus and Aeacus and their retinues. The central chamber of souls has nine entrances, one for each of the petty deaths and their retinues and each without decoration or ornament. Each tunnel-like entrance leads into a triangular pit with a tall throne on a tall pedestal (a narrow set of stairs winds around the circular pedestal to give access to the throne) for the petty death or their representative – the rest of the retinue stand in the pit. A second iron door leads into the pit, through which souls collected in the harbor below are sent to be collected by the proper petty death. Most of the souls are simple enough to categorize, but a few spark great debates and shouting matches between the deaths and their retinues, debates which are then voted on by the three judges, their words being final. The judges sit atop a central pillar, each in their own throne. The pillar can be rotated by a team of zombie giants at the direction of the bailiff, a tall, angelic figure of grim humor wearing robes of copper and black and carrying a golden shield and sword.

## 2303.

A tall, crooked pillar stands in a crossroads here. Sitting on the pillar there is a skeleton holding a golden ear horn. Should one ask it directions to a location, it will lean down a bit holding the horn to its skull. One will have to climb 10 feet up the pole to be heard, at which point it will point its bony finger in the direction they wish to go. The skeleton has a mere 3 hit points and is easily destroyed, but will re-assemble itself the next morning and climb back on the pillar.

## 2308.

A village of 200 miners of the embalmer culture dwells here in a number of thatched huts nestled between two foreboding limestone karst ridges. The miners are insular and rude, and react violently to visitors until given a demonstration of their power. During the daytime, the miners are to be found digging into one of the ridges, expanding the natural limestone caves therein following iron deposits. They prepare the stone by building great fires with the twisted white trees that fill the gaps between the ridges. This causes the stone to crack, making it easier to pick apart. The miners refine some of the iron themselves, turning it into tools, weapons and armor. The remainder is passed on to their king in Hex 2409. The village is ruled by a blustering reeve called Kopos, a black-bearded giant with a glass jaw. He commands 10 soldiers armored in chainmail and armed with shield, javelins, short sword and dagger. The miners fight with picks and slings if called to do so.

**Kopos the Reeve: HD 4 (13 hp); AC 4 [15]; Atk 1 weapon (1d10); Move 12; Save 13; CL/XP 4/120; Special: None.**

## 2405.

Gangs of 1d8 strange children might be discovered in this valley of brambles. There are 32 children in all. They are scrawny little things, with gray, almost translucent skin, knobby knees and elbows and large, pleading eyes. The children are actually immature doppelgangers. The infant doppelgangers have miniscule filaments on their fingertips. By touching a person (they have surprisingly strong grasps) they absorb the life force from a person, growing larger as they do so and taking on the person's appearance and memories. Each round an infant doppelganger maintains a grapple, it drains one level from its victim, adding it to its own total. Each level drawn from a magic user carries with it 1d6 spell levels worth of spells, while clerics simply lose 1d6 spell levels of spells. When fully grown to 4 Hit Dice, the now mature doppelganger releases its weakened victim (who must save or fall into a sleep for 1 hour per lost level) and departs the hidden valley for the wide world beyond. The children live in little hollowed out areas within the brambles, and here one might find an odd bit of treasure or two scavenged from kills.

## 2409.

This hex holds a cliff city of the embalmers overlooking meadows of grayish-green grass grazed on by sheep. The wool of the sheep and rams is black on the right side and white on the left. The city is populated by about 2,000 people. The embalmers are sheep herders, raising them for their wool, milk, cheese and meat. The highest caste among the people is the herdsmen – even the king keeps a herd looked over by young men attached to his court – followed by the priests and philosophers and then the warriors. Male embalmers keep the herds, shear the wool, butcher the animals (never before their third year), milk them and prepare the cheeses while the women weave. The food of the embalmers comes almost entirely from the sheep and from the fields of gray wheat grown in the highlands surrounding their cliff city. A typical meal includes stewed hog and mutton, blocks of powerful smelling cheese and large, round loaves of gray, unleavened bread made of wheat and bone meal and topped with a drizzle of grease and a dab of butter.

The embalmer priests wear black robes and weave black beads into their hair and beards. Priestly men embalm the dead and sing their hymns while priestly women weave their hair of corpses into carpets, cloaks and slippers, dying these articles with extracted humors and turning them into magic items. They wear wicker holy symbols and learn to command the undead, rather than destroy them. They primarily pray to Ingueas [Hex 1102], but also pay homage to Gohl [Hex 0502]. The temple of the embalmers is placed adjacent to the palace, high on the cliffs and fronted with a large set of double doors of black, glossy wood inlaid with silver. The priests trill on bagpipes in their rituals, and two priests are always in attendance at court to announce their visitors (and purify the throne room due to their foreign presence) with these pipes.

The king of the cliffs is Svarius, a swarthy, stock bull of a man with bright, violet eyes and a curled blue-black beard. He wears a magic cloak and magic slippers woven from corpse hair and necklaces of the bronzed teeth of his fallen enemies. On his chest is a golden pectoral, on his head an iron crown with gilded ram horns. Svarius' palace occupies a full third of the cliff dwelling and secret passages provide him access to many of the homes of his people. Every room of the palace is covered in bas reliefs of manticores, serpents, warriors, scorpion demons and other strange creatures locked in battle or groveling at the feet of a king with a blue-black beard and diamond eyes. Under the palace there is a furnace that sends heat through the hollow floors and walls, fueled by sheep dung and the bodies of dead peasants. The throne room measures 20 feet in width and 40 feet in length and is tiled in alabaster and lapis lazuli, the vaulted ceiling held aloft by pillars of brass engraved with pomegranate trees and bloated toads. Barred windows line the walls of the throne room. The windows connect to tiny alcoves in which reside mummified philosophers and kings, the privy council of Svarius. Svarius throne is made of blackened wrought iron and surrounded by large, golden pillows for the members of his court. His wife, Queen Sulani, stands behind the throne, whispering words of advice while her fingers sooth her husband's brow. Sulani is taller than her husband, with a harshly beautiful, angular face and strong lips colored deep purple. Like most embalmer women, she lightens her skin with special oils. She wears flowing gowns of spider silk and wears beads of gold, silver and precious stones in her long, blue-black hair. The palace rests at the highest level of the cliff city and is fronted by broad terraces supporting gardens of anemones and long lily ponds inhabited by sleek fresh water rays with silvery skin. The walls of these terraces are crenellated to allow for a defense by archers.

The mummies of the embalmers should not be confused with those of the ancient Egyptians or Incas. In the embalmer culture, a corpse is initially prepared in a way similar to the Egyptians, using a fragrant oils and a conglomeration of herbs in a secret formula. After steeping in this formula, the skin of the mummy peels away. Its organs are then removed and placed in funerary urns. The corpse is them methodically dipped in beeswax, the color of the wax depending on its rank and position in life, with a deep purple-crimson wax being used for kings and a saffron wax for philosophers. A jet imbroglio depicting the corpse as it looked in life is placed under the tongue, it is dressed in flowing robes of black, a gold, conical hat is placed on its head and the ritual to animate the corpse then takes place. The corpse is animated in its closet to keep it from spreading mummy rot to the priests. The closet also contains the mummy's organs in their ceramic jars and other regalia important to it in life.

**Embalmer Warrior (200):** HD 1; AC 4 [15]; Atk 1 weapon (1d8); Move 12; Save 17; CL/XP 1/15; Special: None.

**Embalmer Priest (20):** HD 3; AC 4 [15]; Atk 1 weapon (1d8); Move 12; Save 14; CL/XP 4/120; Special: Cast cleric spells, turn undead.

**Mummy:** HD 6+4 (40 hp); AC 3 [16]; Atk Fist (1d12); Move 6; Save 11; CL/XP 7/600; Special: Rot, only hit by magical weapons.

**Queen Sulani:** HD 2 (9 hp); AC 9 [10]; Atk 1 dagger (1d4); Move 12; Save 16; CL/XP 2/30; Special: Cast spells as 1st level magic-user.

**King Svarius:** HD 6 (35 hp); AC 2 [17]; Atk 1 mace (1d8); Move 9; Save 11; CL/XP 6/400; Special: None.

## 2415.

A forest of giant stinkhorn mushrooms grows in this hex. The mushrooms stand anywhere from three to eight feet in height, with pink, irregular stalks and topped with what appear to be six or seven tendrils colored coral and white. The tops are covered in a sticky slime that smells truly awful (per the troglodyte stench ability). The slime attracts the attention of giant flies, who buzz around the stinkhorns. Adventurers picking their way through the forest have a 2 in 6 chance of being attacks by 1d6 giant flies. Those who touch the slime will find themselves covered with the mushroom's spores. Within one day, the spores grow into what look like bowling ball sized eggs in 24 hours, and then in 24 more hours sprout into full-sized giant stinkhorns. The eggs are easily removed, so the rapid growth shouldn't threaten anyone's life.

**Giant Flies:** HD 1+1; AC 6 [13]; Atk 1 bite (1d4); Move 12 (F18); Save 17; CL/XP 1/15; Special: Bite has 10% chance of causing disease (save negates).

## 2511.

On a steep hillside you come across a herd of rams and sheep. The animals are black on one side and white on the other and have horns the color of dusty sunbeams. The animals are herded by a young embalmer in long, turquoise colored robes, saffron slippers and a traditional, horn-shaped head covering, also of saffron. The lad carries a spear and sling and a ram's horn is slung around his chest and a golden stone, round, is hung around his neck on a leather thong. The boy is accompanied by his sheepdog. He is currently trying to extract a strange, silvery object from a narrow crevasse. The object is ovoid in shape and the merest touch causes the skin to turn white and sends an anemic feeling rushing through one's body (saving throw or constitution reduced by half, with lost constitution returning at the rate of one point per day). The object is something akin to an egg, holding within it what can only be described as an anti-phoenix, a bird shrouded in freezing mists that eventually turns into ice and, once it melts, reveals a new egg hidden within its body. Once hatched, the anti-phoenix grows quickly, reaching full size within three days and three nights, and then goes on a rampage of destruction. Once the creature has absorbed 1,001 souls, it finds a tall mountain top and turns to ice, gradually melting over the course of 100 years.

**Anti-Phoenix:** HD 12 (60 hp); AC 2 [17]; Atk 2 talons (2d6), beak (3d6+level drain); Move 12 (F24); Save 3; CL/XP 16/3200; Special: Drain 1 level with beak, immunity to cold, magic resistance (25%), +2 or better weapon to hit.

## 2603.

A canyon cuts through the mountains here, the walls of the canyon composed of glassy quartz and an icy stream rushing through it. Desperate men formed of magma attempt to climb from the cold river, but find it impossible to scale the slick cliffs.

## 2607.

The stronghold of Egygddedrol, one of the nine petty deaths, is located in this hex. The stronghold is a pit, inky black, 300 feet in diameter and 500 feet deep. At the bottom of the pit there is a dome of black glass, shiny and cool. The dome can only easily be entered (but not exited) by shades and those invited by Egygddedrol. Invaders can bypass the glossy dome with a *wish* spell or similar magic.

Within the dome, the stronghold takes the form of three levels of chambers and hallways, all composed of the same glossy substance and all hard right angles. Shades wander the halls taking their frustration out on corporeal visitors, angry that they may never escape the dome and reach the earthbound heaven. The main servants of Egygddedrol are kobolds with gray and black scales and long, white beards sprouting from their chins. These kobolds are aware of the hidden spaces between the walls in the fortress. One can only enter these spaces via concealed magic portals and they can only enter by closing their eyes and holding their breath. The kobolds are avoided by the shades, and they primarily work as wall polishers, disposers of dead adventurers, collectors of discarded loot and soldiers of the petty death. The kobolds wear silvery hide armor and carry poisoned swords and throwing knives (save or paralyzed for 1d4 rounds). Besides kobolds and shades, one can find other incorporeal undead and strange traps in the chambers of the dome.

Among the chambers of the upper level of the dome there are three magic pools that allow access to the middle level. One pool is silver in color, another gold and the last a dull, iron gray. People in possession of the aforementioned metals will find the surface of the pools rubbery but not yielding. Discarded metals are gathered by the dome's kobold servants.

In the center of the middle level of the dome there is a large, round chamber with a vaulted ceiling. Hanging in the middle of this chamber is what appears to be a black sun. The surface of the sun is always agitated, sending arcs of black flame throughout the chamber. The sun is terribly cold, and every minute spent in the room inflicts one point of cold damage to those not properly attired. Within 10 feet of the sun, all metal is affected per the spell *chill metal* and damage increases to 1d4 per minute. To pass to the lowest level of the dome, one must plunge themselves into the black sun, suffering 1d6 points of cold damage.

Those who enter the black sun will find themselves in one of four circular rooms, sitting unclothed and unequipped in a shallow pool of chilly water. Above them, the ceiling is covered with a mosaic representing a black sun. Two doors exit these rooms, leading into the labyrinthine passages of the lower level, all of which lead inexorably to the grand central chamber wherein Egygddedrol sits enthroned.

Egygddedrol takes the form of a tall, leggy, mature woman with bright, yellow skin and a multitude of writhing arms. One of these arms carries a round, black shield held horizontally like a platter. Upon the shield there sits a blood red apple. As notable as this shield and apple are her eyes. Both are large and round, but one is as black as night and the other as brilliant as the sun. Egygddedrol's temple contains a pit of green fire that flickers with unnatural sloth and tend to entrance those who are weak of will. The walls of the temple, unlike those of the rest of the dome, are ancient, pitted white limestone. The green fire casts long shadows against the walls, and Egygddedrol can animate these shadows to attack with the power of stone giants.

As one enters the temple, the petty goddess, standing on the other side of the fire, will glare at the intruders with her awful eyes. She will say, in a voice commanding and melodic "What will you have of me?"

Should one request the soul of a loved one, she will command them to step through the green flames. Those who do so must roll 1d20 and compare the result to their wisdom score. A person who rolls higher than their wisdom score by less than their own level is granted the soul they seek, and that soul is restored to corporeal form. A person who rolls higher than their wisdom, but by more than their level are granted an audience with the requested soul in the form of a shade, and are given the opportunity to pass into the underworld with that shade. A person who rolls beneath their wisdom suffers the loss of

one level for every point of difference and is granted nothing but a dismissive laugh.

Should one request any other favor from the goddess, they will be asked to step forward and taste her apple. A similar roll to that described above must be made, the result compared to their constitution. One who rolls above their constitution by less than their level is granted this boon (within reason). Those who roll above their constitution but by more than their level are granted the boon they seek, but their soul is given over to the petty death. Such a person suffers a -1 penalty to all saving throws against death and forfeits the chance of being returned to life after death. Those who roll beneath their constitution drop dead on the spot, their shades floating up from their bodies and into the pit of green fire.

Egygddedrol's eyes can project cones of energy that project portals against walls. Her white eye can send petitioners back to the world above, while her black eye can send them to planes and world's beyond. Egygddedrol claims the souls of explorers and seekers of knowledge.

**Egygddedrol: HD 14 (75 hp); AC -1 [20]; Atk 4 strikes (1d6+1) or spells; Move 30; Save 3; CL/XP 20/4400; Special: +1 or better weapon to hit, casts spells as a 10th level cleric, immune to fear and all undead attacks and abilities, command undead as 20th level cleric, animate shadows, open portals with eyes.**

## 2618.

A gang of lacedons (aquatic ghouls) that look like squat men and women with gray, blotchy skin and bloated faces with rotted away noses bathe in the moonlight on the shore. 3d6 lacedons will be encountered, some of them feasting on recently arrived corpses. One lacedon wears a platinum pectoral decorated with images of coatls. The lacedon is worth 1,200 gp.

**Lacedon: HD 2; AC 6 [13]; Atk 2 claws (1d3), bite (1d4); Move 9; Save 16; CL/XP 3/60; Special: Immunities, paralysis, breath water.**

## 2713.

A weird, bloated, silvery animal like a hairless bear crossed with a puffer fish has its foot caught in a steel trap. The beast is being tormented by five imps with flaming brands. If released, the beast floats into the heavens and each rescuer finds a ceramic token in their pouch or pocket. These tokens can be crushed or broken, summoning a single moon bear to their aid for 6 rounds.

**Imp: HD 2; AC 2 [17]; Atk 1 sting (1d4+poison); Move 6 (F16); Save 16; CL/XP 6/400; Special: Poison tail, polymorph, regenerate, immune to fire.**

**Moon Bear: HD 7 (21 hp); AC 0 [19]; Atk 1 touch (1d6 frost+poison); Move 18; Save 9; CL/XP 11/1700; Special: Poison (save or have 1 point of wisdom per day turned into a point of charisma, wisdom cannot go below 3 nor charisma above 18), immunity to cold, magic resistance (30%).**

## 2716.

A night hag called Hepzibah and mounted on a nightmare is leading a caravan of three white wagons pulled by white oxen and driven by goblins with blue skin and swathed in white wraps and wearing necklaces of human teeth around their necks (they believe the necklaces protect them from humans). Inside each wagon there are glass jugs packed in rags. Each jug appears to be empty save for a mild glow. These jars contain souls, extracted through a process known only to the night hags. The hags trade them upriver to the great tower in Hex 2205. The essences, when consumed, act as potions: Choleric humors make one quick to anger and acts as a *potion of lightning bolt* (3 dice bolt, erupts from one's mouth when first they speak words of anger); Melancholic humors make one despondent and act as a *potion of slow*; Phlegmatic humors make one unemotional and act as a *potion of remove curse*; Sanguine humors make one amorous and act as a *potion of charm person*.

Hepzibah currently has one of each vial on her person. The goblins carry daggers and pellet bows. Possessed of sublime calm, these goblins are immune to fear and enjoy a +5 bonus to save vs. mind-affecting spells.

**Goblin Driver:** HD 1d6 (4 hp); AC 6 [13]; Atk 1 weapon (1d6); Move 9; Save 18; CL/XP B/10; Special: None.

**Nightmare:** HD 7 (30 hp); AC -4 [23]; Atk 1 bite (1d8), 2 hoofs (2d6); Move 18 (F35); Save 9; CL/XP 10/1400; Special: Breathe smoke, become incorporeal.

**Hepzibah, Night Hag:** HD 8 (35 hp); AC 8 [11]; Atk 1 bite (2d6); Move 10; Save 8; CL/XP 11/1700; Special: Magic resistance (65%), +2 or better weapon to hit, magical abilities.

## 2804.

The ground gives way here into a deep chasm. The chasm begins narrowly, the entrance appearing to have been carved by a rushing rivulet that is now dry (though there is a 5% chance that it will be flowing after or during a strong rain). Climbing into the chasm is quite treacherous for non-thieves, and requires spikes and ropes and still might take the better part of a day to accomplish safely. The chasm is formed of basalt and is devoid of all life save a stinging insect (distracting, imposes a -1 penalty to all d20 rolls while in the chasm). The chasm runs narrow for about half a mile and then begins to widen, with shallow, stagnant pools of water (or fresh pools, if it is raining) often blocking one's progress. The ground here is often covered in a layer of black sand which sometimes (each traveler must pass a saving throw, +2 if using a 10-ft pole) gives way to pockets of quicksand that can swallow a person in a single round.

This quicksand not only suffocates, but also desiccates a body, inflicting 1d4 points of damage each round. One might discover a dried corpse in these pockets. About one and one half miles into the chasm, from either end, travelers finally come upon the shores of a shallow, black lake. The lake bubbles slightly, releasing a sickening sweet odor into the air that proves mildly intoxicating to halflings (saving throw or exhibit drunkenness). Floating over the lake and gibbering incessantly are 1d4+1 allips. The allips seem drawn to the center of the lake as though moths to a flame, but likewise are unable to approach the exact center of the lake. Lying about 7 feet below the surface of the lake, at its center (the lake measures 200 feet in diameter) is a crystal skull. The skull attracts all undead within 120 feet, but also creates a barrier that undead creatures with fewer than 6 HD cannot pass, and which more powerful undead can only pass if they succeed at a saving throw with a -3 penalty. The bearer of the skull can, once per day, attempt to command undead within 120 feet as though a cleric. Non-clerics make their command undead check as though 2nd level clerics, while clerics make their check as though 2 levels higher.

**Allip:** HD 4; AC 5 [14]; Atk 1 strike (no damage, 1d4 points of wisdom lost); Move F6; Save 13; CL/XP 7/600; Special: Drains wisdom, hypnosis.

## 2810.

A herd of 1d10+10 wild, carnivorous mountain ponies with shaggy coats and wolf-like teeth roam the high meadows here. They are not easily domesticated.

**Carnivorous Pony:** HD 1+1; AC 7 [12]; Atk 1 bite (1d4); Move 18; Save 16; CL/XP 2/30; Special: None.

## 2903.

A band of six dark valkyries, tall, pale women with fiery, golden hair and very high, pronounced cheek bones, is patrolling this hex on their pteranodon mounts. They are seeking one of their number who crept away in the night with a magical sword. The valkyries are armed with barbed harpoons. On any attack roll with this weapon that beats the victim's AC by more than 5, the barbs of the harpoon dig into their flesh. The valkyrie can then slowly (10 feet per round) pull them closer or yank the barbs out of their flesh, inflicting 1d6 points of damage. The escaped valkyrie, called Gjalla, has dug herself a hideout amidst the trees of the forest. She is loathe to leave her hiding place, but will do so to confront any who approach too close. Gjalla wishes to quit the land beyond the Black River and journey into the southern lands as an adventurer.

**Pteranodon:** HD 8 (32 hp each); AC 4 [15]; Atk 2 claws (1d6), bite (2d6); Move 6 (F18); Save 8; CL/XP 9/1100; Special: None.

**Dark Valkyrie:** HD 8 (45 hp); AC 4 [15]; Atk Longsword (1d8); Move 12; Save 8; CL/XP 8/800; Special: *Cause fear* 1/day, turn undead as 8th level cleric.

## 2914.

You discover a vast field of stone pillars, conical in shape and standing 9 feet in height. A hole in the top of each stone emits a steady stream of reddish water, sickening sweet, which feeds a growth of giant sundews around the base of the stone. The stones are placed about twenty feet apart, and the ground between the stones is covered in a reddish muck that supports tangled networks of spurge. The field of stones is 3-miles in radius, centered on the center of the hex. At odd intervals of the day or night, a giant female form appears in the midst of the field, seemingly materializing out of thin air. The giantess (a titan, actually) surveys the lands around the strange garden and casts giant sundew seeds from a leather sack on her hip. She is clothed in a bluish-purple mist and has a thick mane of black hair that falls to the small of her back. The titan, called Chloe, knows something of the secrets of this strange realm, though her reasons for visiting it or tending this garden she will not speak of.

**Giant Sundew:** HD 3; AC 6 [13]; Atk 4 tentacles (1d3+glue); Move 0; Save 14; CL/XP 3/60; Special: Those struck by the creature's tentacles are stuck fast, escaping with an open doors check.

**Chloe, Titan:** HD 18 (80 hp); AC 1 [18]; Atk 1 weapon (2d8); Move 21; Save 3; CL/XP 20/4400; Special: Spells (2 magic-user spells per level from 1st to 7th, 2 cleric spells per level from 1st to 7th).

## 3011.

Amidst the white woods you spy the shattered remains of a hall. What remains of the hall are three walls of gray stone with a large meteorite lodged in the tiled floor. What remains of the lord of this feast hall lie underneath this meteor, which was summoned by a disgruntled old woman, a worker in magic, who was refused entry into the hall. The lord's knights were transformed into a pack of carrion wolves with patchy fur and gaunt builds that still haunt the ruins (4 in 6 chance of encountering 4d4 wolves each day one spends in the ruins). The guests of the lord, stuffing their faces with sweets and savories while the old woman went hungry, were burnt to a cinder in the meteoric conflagration and rose as three cinder ghouls who rise like smoke from the floor if the meteor is touched. The lord's body was crushed and burned – only a few fragments of charred bone remain – but his *ring of shooting stars* can still be found lodged in the rock.

**Carrion Wolf:** HD 2+2; AC 7 [12]; Atk 1 bite (1d4+1); Move 18; Save 16; CL/XP 2/30; Special: None.

**Cinder Ghoul:** HD 8; AC 0 [19]; Atk 1 strike (1d8+1d6 fire+level drain); Move F15; Save 8; CL/XP 13/2300; Special: +1 or better weapon to hit, drains 1 level with hit (save negates), immune to fire, can take smoke form (as *gaseous form*), force smoke into opponent's lungs (save or suffer 1d4 points of damage per round for 1d4+1 rounds).

## 3017.

The remnants of villa are carved into the sides of a crater. A tangled vineyard of black grapes grows thick on the crater floor. The grapes of the vineyard are mildly narcotic and used to make a black wine favored throughout the region. The villa is now home to a ragged band of halflings. The halflings look like chubby children with wide grins, sparkling eyes and fingers and toes stained black from the grapes. Deep purple pseudo-dragons also live amongst the vines, sometimes frolicking with the halflings, other times tormenting them. The halflings feast on the grapes and on the giant rats that crawl out of the ground to sample the vines at night. These rats are split down the middle and filled with a stuffing of mushrooms and grape skins and then roasted.

## 3101.

Wihiedro might be the most wicked of the petty deaths. She appears as a wide-hipped crone with pallid skin and slitted, blue eyes that burn with malevolence. Wihiedro's forehead is large and domed, her silver hair hangs in long, thick braids. She wears no clothing and carries a *+2 herculean club* bound in bands of studded bronze. Wihiedro is surrounded by an aura of menace that claws at the hearts of decent people (lawful and neutral characters must pass a saving throw or become bestial in manner and desire, turning into trolls in a number of rounds equal to their wisdom scores divided by 3). Trolls and ogres in Wihiedro's presence cannot resist her commands.

Wihiedro dwells in a massive, cavernous vault with a roaring court of 20 ogres and 10 trolls, all especially large and savage specimens. In the center of their court there is a circle of silver, 20 feet in diameter, into which the shades of the wicked and false are thrown. Inside the circle, the shades take a semi-corporeal form and can be tormented by the whips and stones of the giants.

Wihiedro - Goddess of evil, she takes the form of a tall, wide-hipped crone – the matron made barren with time – with pallid skin and slitted, blue eyes and a domed forehead. Wihiedro wears no clothing and carries a herculean club topped with bands of bronze. Wihiedro is served by a roaring court of trolls and ogres. She is surrounded by an aura of malice that claws at the hearts of decent people. She claims the souls of the wicked and false.

**Wihiedro: HD 15 (85 hp); AC -1 [20]; Atk 1 *+2 club* (1d12+1); Move 9; Save 3; CL/XP 18/3800; Special: Only harmed by +1 or better weapons, immune to fear and cold, aura of menace, command trolls and ogres.**

## 3109.

On the terraced hillsides of a tall hillock there is a settlement of hidden people called skulks. The skulks are naturally invisible. They grow vines of jasmine, feeding on their scents each night. The skulks know many secrets (1d6 rumors) and will trade them for a blood oath to rid the land of the petty deaths. The skulks precede their coming to the land beyond the Black Water and relish the day when they are no more.

**Skulk: HD 2; AC 6 [13]; Atk 1 weapon (1d6); Move 12; Save 17; CL/XP 2/30; Special: Surprise on 1-4 on 1d6.**

## 3113.

As the adventurers walk through the woods, they notice the trees becoming more angular, the branches coming out at right angles to the trunk and the leaves becoming perfect, silvery circles. Eventually they come to a path of silver bricks (no, not real silver). As one proceeds down the path, they trees begin to display carvings of angelic faces. White owls are seen roosting in the branches and silver foxes lurk on the edges of the path. One finally comes to a golden stair that seems to ascend into the gray heavens. The stairs are actually an illusion, being composed of dingy gray stone and descending rather than ascending. When one reaches the "top" of the stairs, they will believe they are looking out at a celestial meadow of unicorns and golden-throated cranes. In fact, they have arrived in a vast slaughter house. The slaughter house is run by a gang of eight minotaurs, who process their victims into fat sausages and bags of bone meal.

**Minotaur: HD 6+4; AC 6 [13]; Atk 1 butt (2d4), bite (1d3), weapon (1d8); Move 12; Save 11; CL/XP 6/400; Special: Never lost in mazes.**

## 3120.

A chalk pyramid of the stepped variety lies at the center of a village of 200 ghuls. The ghuls live in burrows dug around the perimeter of the pyramid. At the top of the pyramid there is a cistern. A silver statue of a woman in a robes and holding aloft a sword is submerged in the temple, the upper portion of the sword rising above the surface of the water. The ghuls avoid the upper portion of the pyramid and seem to fear silver, though it does not particular harm to them. The ghuls live as hunters and gatherers on the steppe, their main prey being, of course, the zombies that seek the earthbound paradise or any living creatures foolish enough to wander the land beyond the Black Water. They are led by a council of elders, three men and a woman who wear black robes and multi-colored mantles and have large, wooden hoops in their ears. Like most ghuls, the people of the village have skin the color of tallow that is drawn tight over their thin, unwholesome frames. Their lips are pulled back from their large teeth and their noses are tiny and pointed. The hunters of the tribe carry short bows and curved short swords and wear leather armor. The ghul's treasure, kept in a secret chamber in their pyramid, consists of 515 large gold coins (worth 6 gp each).

**Ghul Warrior: HD 1; AC 7 [12]; Atk 1 weapon (1d6) or strike (1d3 plus stun); Move 12; Save 17; CL/XP 2/30; Special: Touch stuns (save negates) for 1d3 rounds.**

## 3204.

Emntrix, the petty death that claims the soul of soldiers and servants, keeps a vast training yard here. She has complete control of the environment within the yard, being able to bring wind and rain into it, cause pillars of earth to rise suddenly from the ground or crevasses to run like rivers across it, etc. In this mile wide yard she conducts mock battles, much to the chagrin of the shades under her charge, who only wish a moment of peace after lives of war and toil. The walls of the yard are 30 feet thick and 70 feet tall, and taper from top to base. Narrow doors of thick glass, 25 feet tall, grant access to the yard and are placed in the four cardinal directions. The doors only open for warriors, though non-warriors can follow a warrior into the yard.

Emntrix is a 9-ft tall woman with the tail of a scorpion, her body covered by a glossy black carapace, over which she wears blue, gladiator-style armor, her helm surmounted by a black horsehair crest, her breastplate bearing the image of scorpion. Her arms are clad in dozens of bronze bangles and bracelets (worth a total of 100 gp) and she carries a *+2 warhammer* that seems to absorb light. The warhammer claims the soul of any warrior it slays, rejecting the souls of non-warriors.

Emntrix is always found at the center of her battles, for they are done for her amusement alone. At noon and midnight, a great bell is rung and the battle stops. At this point, a stooped figure of a man makes his way across the battlefield carrying a goblet of wine on a tray and a stool for his mistress, that she may take refreshment. The man is Ravensworth, her valet and butler. He is dressed in a black velvet doublet and trousers, with plentiful lace ruffles and carries a simple dagger.

**Ravensworth: HD 4 (16 hp); AC 6 [13]; Atk 1 dagger (1d4); Move 12; Save 13; CL/XP 6/400; Special: Back attack – save or death.**

**Emntrix: HD 16 (100 hp); AC -3 [22]; Atk 1 weapon (1d8+2) or sting (1d6 plus poison); Move 15; Save 3; CL/XP 19/4100; Special: Only harmed by +1 or better weapons, immune to fear, gaze causes warriors to go berserk unless they pass a saving throw; berserkers are +1 to hit and damage and attack random targets for 1d3+3 rounds.**

## 3402.

Uddeso, the petty death of famine who claims the souls of people who have died unfulfilled, dwells in this hex in a stronghold of black towers. There are eight towers in all, seven smaller outer towers surrounding a larger central tower. The arched ceiling of each tower is illuminated in gold and silver paint, depicting gaunt, drawn saints living in barred cells and visited by all manner of strange animals.

The outer towers are stocked with piles and piles of food – barrels of nuts, heaps of fruit and vegetables, joints of beef and mutton hanging from hooks, loaves of bread in every imaginable shape, etc. All of this food looks delectable, but turns to ashes in one's mouth.

The central tower is the court of Uddeso, a black-skinned woman with a narrow build and the sunken in eyes of a corpse. Uddeso wears scale armor composed of glossy, red hexagons stitched together with sinews on a backing of leather made from the footpads of pilgrims who died before reaching their destination. She carries a bronze buckler that bears half a human skull and *+1 godentag* (a sort of spiked club common to rebellious peasant armies) that invokes a hunger so terrible in the creatures it touches that they must pass a saving throw or spend the next 1d6 rounds scavenging for food. Victims who fail their saving throws by more than 6 points will be possessed with a cannibalistic hunger. The walls of the central tower are covered with hundreds of perches for a vast murder of crows, the servants of Uddeso.

**Murder of Crows: HD 2; AC 4 [15]; Atk 1 swarm (1d4+eye gouge); Move 6 (F18); Save 16; CL/XP 4/120; Special: Those struck by swarm have a 1 in 20 chance of losing an eye each round (save negates), those in the swarm must save each round or be struck by confusion, murder takes half damage from edged and piercing weapons.**

**Uddeso: HD 13 (88 hp); AC -3 [22]; Atk *+1 godentag* (1d10+1); Move 12; Save 3; CL/XP 19/4100; Special: Only harmed by +1 or better weapons, casts spells as a 7th level cleric, immune to fear, hold person gaze attack (2/day).**

## 3407.

Beneath the white boughs of the woodlands there is a cottage of stone with a roof of slate. Just beyond the cottage there is a large clearing planted with platinum blonde wheat and rows of caraway. The cottage is owned by an annis hag, who plows her own field with the help of a haggard draft horse – a polymorphed magic-user who made the mistake of collapsing on her doorstep. The hag uses her crops to bake cookies cut in pleasing shapes and flavored with bitter crystals – the crystallized frustrations of shades caught in the willows that surround the house. The cookies, when placed under the tongue, make on invisible to undead creatures. If swallowed, they are a deadly poison. The hag trades the cookies to adventurers in return for favors..

**Annis Hag: HD 8 (36 hp); AC 1 [18]; Atk 2 claws (2d8), 1 bite (1d8); Move 12; Save 8; CL/XP 10/1400; Special: Hug and rend, polymorph, call mists.**

## 3413.

A band of intelligent opossums, bandits wearing leather armor and carrying long knives lurk in the treetops. The marsupial bandits have long, prehensile tails and nasty little teeth. There are 20 of the bandits present. They keep their treasure, 680 gp and a brass medallion (worth 700 gp, proclaims one as "#1"), in a leather sack hidden in the boughs of a tree. The opossums speak in throaty, whispery growls and wear black masks.

**Opossum Bandits: HD 1d6; AC 7 [12]; Atk 1 knife (1d4) or bite (1d4 plus disease); Move 12 (C9); Save 18 (16 vs. disease); CL/XP 1/15; Special: Disease, surprise on 1-3 on 1d6.**

## 3517.

A tribe of 200 carrion orcs dwells here grass huts. The orcs have the faces of boars, with oversized tusks – some of which growing up through their own noses. They are especially brutish, wearing furs and pelts (+1 bonus to AC) and carrying clubs and cast off weapons. Among the orcs there are three sub-chiefs (2 HD each) and a large leader with an iron fist (literally – its hand has been replaced by a iron fist that strikes as a heavy mace). The leader is called Grubrut. Within his iron fist there is an entrapped soul in a crystal bubble. The spirit belonged to a temptress, and it now whispers in Grubrut's ear, trying to turn him into a great leader who can eventually return her to a corporeal existence in some other woman's body. The orcs have a single guard beast who serves as their "totem" as well – a tigrilla chained to a tall post. Captives are thrown to the tigrilla as an offering, as are wounded orcs. The orcs possess 2,700 sp and 1,410 gp

**Orcs: HD 1; AC 6 [13]; Atk 1 weapon (1d8); Move 12; Save 17; CL/XP 1/15; Special: None.**

**Grubrut: HD 6 (26 hp); AC 3 [16]; Atk 1 weapon (1d8+2); Move 9; Save 11; CL/XP 6/400; Special: None. Wears a brass chain worth 145 gp.**

**Tigrilla: HD 5 (30 hp); AC 5 [14]; Atk 1 bite (2d6), 2 claws (1d8); Move 15 (Climb 9); Save 12; CL/XP 5/240; Special: Rake with claws for double damage if both claw attacks hit in same round.**

## 3521.

This hex is covered by a thick carpet of sargassum. Two large galleasses, once vessels of the imperial navy of the northern men, have been stuck in the weeds for decades. The crews (both 25 strong), now skeletons, roar challenges at one another, launching whatever bits of ordnance at one another they can with crude, creaking catapults. The skeletons are clad in rags and bits of shrunken leather armor. They wield curved swords (rusty, -1 to hit and damage) and short bows (warped, -1 to hit). The holds of both ships are empty. Both captain's quarters are inhabited by poltergeists. One contains 1,920 sp and 520 gp in a terracotta basin (itself worth 100 gp) and the other 1,500 sp, 540 gp and two massive rock crystals (300 gp each) in a locked sea chest.

**Skeleton: HD 1; AC 8 [11]; Atk 1 weapon (1d6); Move 12; Save 18; CL/XP 1/15; Special: None.**

**Poltergeist: HD 2; AC 7 [12]; Atk throw object (fear); Move 3 (F6); Save 16; CL/XP 5/240; Special: Fear, telekinesis, natural invisibility.**

## 3609.

Amidst the White Woods there is an expansive grove so terrible as to force one to question the sanity of Creation. The grove consists of trees much thicker of trunk and branched of bough than the silvery beeches that fill the White Wood. These trees exhibit a color reminiscent of pale flesh, and in fact their outer bark is a thick skin, not unlike that of a rhinoceros. Within the tree's epidermis is thick, dense flesh (tastes something like bitter chicken) and an inner core of bone. The fruit of the tree looks like bright red jujubes covered in something approximating human skin and filled with a bloody pulp. Large, dangerous swine wander this terrible forest, feasting on fallen fruits and savaging any living or undead thing that crosses their path – such encounters occur on a roll of 1 on 1d6 made each hour. Besides the swine, the forests only inhabitants are its dryads, if true dryads they can be considered. The dryads of the fleshy wood are tall and rubenesque, with honey-red hair and ruddy skin and purple lips that are full and inviting. The dryads carry leather pouches of blood wine that they share willingly with travelers, who must take care not to become intoxicated lest they succumb to vampiric urges and, at the next full moon find themselves transformed into one of the swine of the fleshy forest. It should be noted that anyone chopping at one of these trees will perceive a noticeable shudder in the thing, as though reacting silently to wracking pain. Cuts in the trees bleed, and stumps produce a steady flow of blood for several minutes and attract 1d6+1 of the swine within 1 turn.

**Swine:** HD 3+3; AC 7 [12]; Atk 1 gore (2d4); Move 15; Save 14; CL/XP 4/120; Special: Continues attacking 2 rounds after death.

**Dryad:** HD 2; AC 9 [10]; Atk 1 wooden dagger (1d4); Move 12; Save 16; CL/XP 3/60; Special: Charm person at -2 save.

## 3802.

A dusty, abandoned mine shaft burrowed into the limestone mountains here gives access to a vast maze of passages and chambers. The complex was dug by massive, four armed creatures known as kruks, and consist of tall, round chambers connected at varying levels by square tunnels, usually 10 feet tall and wide and running no more than 150 feet. A tunnel one enters from the floor of a chamber might end at ceiling level in another chamber, making the maze a matter of up and down as well as north-south-east-west. The maze is carved from the limestone, though one might also run into veins of schist and marble. Some chambers are partially flooded by underground springs, with a ledge provided around the pool of water to allow bathing and the filling of waterskins. Other chambers contain bronze cages hung from the ceiling by chains that can be raised and lowered via winches. These cages once held prisoners, for the kruks were infamous slavers. Very few of the kruks now dwell in their maze complex, usually in large chambers fortified with iron doors and containing sleeping alcoves and a barred slave pit for their remaining slaves. Such a chamber houses 2d6 kruks and 3d4 slaves (humans, dwarves, elves, etc).

The more worrisome inhabitants of the mazes are minotaurs, dusky-skinned men with the heads of white bulls who devour the living and paint garish designs on the walls with the blood. The kruks are said to know a way through the underworld to the Earthbound Paradise beyond, but others say they merely know of passages that descend ever deeper into the earth.

**Kruk:** HD 6+2; AC 5 [14]; Atk 4 slams (1d6); Move 12; Save 11 (6 vs. spells); CL/XP 7/600; Special: +5 save vs. spells.

**Minotaur:** HD 6+4; AC 6 [13]; Atk 1 head butt (2d4), bite (1d3), weapon (1d8); Move 12; Save 11; CL/XP 6/400; Special: Never gets lost in labyrinths.

## 3805.

The trees in this hex become much larger than most trees in these woods, with bloated white trunks and branches that reach up for the moon and create a canopy at least 300 feet in diameter. Gloomwings place their larvae in these trees, the boughs often being born down by fat, tenebrous worms. The eggs are valued highly by the peoples of the land beyond the Black River for their medicinal value, and although the beasts cannot be tamed the worms are sometimes kept as dangerous guard beasts. Encounters with 1d4 of the worms occur on a roll of 1-4 on 1d6 each day, while encounters with 1d6 gloomwings occur on the roll of 1-2 on 1d6. One of the larger trees in this hex is hollowed, an armored skeleton resting there. The skeleton is not animated, though it can speak with a rough, gravely, tired voice. The skeleton will answer no more than one question per person, and has a good knowledge of this strange land. The skeleton once belonged to an avenging knight, who, set upon by a trio of ravenous worms one night was killed and discovered that his spirit, while not strong enough to animate or escape, was too strong to fade away. Beneath the skeleton there is a small hole that can be expanded by removing a few stones.

This tunnel descends at a steep slope about 100 feet before forking. The left fork of the tunnel leads into a triangular cavern about 40 feet long with the ceiling peaking about 18 feet above the floor, which is roughly 10 feet wide. Thick webs fill this cavern, home to a dozen giant spiders and hiding in their midst a web of silver. This web, when spoken over by certain words of power and traced by a finger anointed with a mixture of wine, honey and grave dirt, allows instant transportation for a magic-user and any holding on to his robe to any

one of the strongholds of the nine petty deaths.

The right fork of the tunnel continues downward, eventually ending in a dusty vault containing thousands of thick, leather bound tomes, each one containing a single large, complicated seal that is the true name of a great soul – kings, queens, wizards, angels, greater demons and dukes of Hell. The librarian of the chamber is a lich, a pathetic looking bag of bones hunched over a simple library table, a dozen books stacked upon it, its bony finger tracing a seal, endeavoring to understand it. The lich, a very old soul called Alu, perhaps the first magician among mankind, will, after some time or if confronted, raise his heavy, cobwebbed head and deal with the intruders. The lich has a treasure of 15,830 sp and 2,550 gp kept in 20 small wooden cubes with no apparent way to open them and a *helm of fiery brilliance* hidden in a cache in the ceiling of the vault.

**Tenebrous Worm:** HD 10; AC 2 [17]; Atk 1 bite (2d6); Move 3; Save 5; CL/XP 12/2000; Special: Acid, poison bristles (paralysis, chance to avoid equal to armor bonus on 1d10).

**Gloomwing:** HD 5; AC 0 [19]; Atk 2 claws (1d4), bite (1d8); Move 3 (F15); Save 12; CL/XP 9/1100; Special: Confusion, implant, weakness pheromone, summon gloomwings.

**Giant Spider:** HD 2+2; AC 6 [13]; Atk 1 bite (1d6+poison); Move 18; Save 16; CL/XP 5/240; Special: Lethal poison, surprise on 1-5 on 1d6.

**Alu, Lich:** HD 18 (89 hp); AC 0 [19]; Atk 1 hand (1d10+paralysis); Move 6; Save 3; CL/XP 21/4700; Special: Appearance causes paralytic fear, touch causes automatic paralysis, spells as 12th level magic-user.

## 3815.

A troupe of seven pallid mystics is making its way across the steppe in search of secrets. Each mystic has the ability to *speak with dead*, and uses it to gather secret from the departed, tattooing these secrets on their own skin in a strange runic alphabet. The mystics are now covered in varying amounts of blue-black ink, which they keep hidden beneath black slops and gabardines and ivory stockings. The mystics cover their platinum hair with floppy felt hats decorated with twisting, twiggy branches in place of feathers. Each mystic wields a curved silver long sword with great skill. The mystics are very protective of their secrets, but are willing to share their knowledge of the lands beyond the Black Water, provided their questioners are willing to pay in silver.

**Mystic Warrior:** HD 9 (50 hp each); AC 2 [17]; Atk 1 sword (1d8+1); Move 15; Save 7; CL/XP 10/1400; Special: *Speak with dead*, always win initiative.

## 3821.

A tribe of 10 merrow (aquatic ogres) and 50 mermaids dwells just beneath the waves here in a massive abalone shell. The material of the shell is stronger than iron. It is divided into a hundred chambers, each entered through a curtain of shells. The mermaids dwell within the shell, only leaving it during what passes for the daytime to brush their hair and seduce passing ships. The mermaids have rounded faces and black, silky skin with golden-red hair. Their eyes are grayish-green and emit a faint light. The merrow are monstrous creatures, with thick, black, scaled skin imprinted with red geometric patterns, gaping mouths and bulbous, cloudy fish eyes. Within the abalone shell the merrow and mermaids have 390 sp, 770 gp and a large tourmaline worth 1,250 gp.

**Mermaid:** HD 1; AC 7 [12]; Atk 1 tail slap (1d4); Move 1 (Swim 18); Save 17; CL/XP 1/15; Special: Breathe water.

**Merrow:** HD 4+1; AC 5 [14]; Atk 1 weapon (1d10+1); Move 9; Save 13; CL/XP 4/120; Special: Breathe water.

# New Monsters

## Basilim

Basilim are warriors that have been petrified by basilisks or sorcerers. Over the centuries, by force of will, they become living statues. Most are quite mad and can save against mental effects every round until they succeed. Many basilim have levels in the fighting-man class, being able to attain the 5th level of experience.

**Basilim: HD 2+2; AC 5 [14]; Atk 2 slams (1d6); Move 9; Save 3; CL/XP 3/60; Special: Madness, half damage from non-magical weapons.**

## Beyonder

Beyonders are semi-humans that dwell on the shores of the land beyond the Black Water. They are tall, hunched humanoids with pallid, hairless skin and yellow eyes devoid of warmth. Beyonders grow their finger and toe nails long and decorate their bodies with triangular metal charms hung on chains that pierce their flesh. They wear multiple layers of clothing and robes, always in dark colors. Beyonder warriors wear scale and ring armor, rarely chainmail, and carry curved swords and daggers. Beyonders care little for material wealth, preferring instead to trade in secrets. For this reason, ignore treasure generated for beyonders that is not in the form of objects, magical or otherwise.

**Common Beyonder: HD 1d6; AC 7 [12]; Atk 1 weapon (1d6); Move 9; Save 18 (14 vs. poison and magic); CL/XP 1/15; Special: Cast one cleric or magic-user spell per day.**

**Beyonder Leader: HD 4d6; AC 7 [12]; Atk 1 weapon (1d6+1); Move 9; Save 13 (9 vs. poison and magic); CL/XP 5/240 or 6/400; Special: Cast cleric and magic-user spells.**

## Bugaboo

Bugaboos are strange constructs composed of a bear's headless body topped by a bronze sphere that resembles a jack-o-lantern. The sphere contains a powerful animating spirit that, if destroyed, destroys the creature. Hitting the bronze sphere requires one to hit and Armor Class of 0 [19], and the sphere can take up to 10 points of damage before it is damaged or knocked off. Damage inflicted on the sphere does not count against the creature's total damage. Creatures with 3 or fewer Hit Dice must save vs. fear when they see a bugaboo or flee for a number of rounds equal to their constitution score divided by 3, thereafter falling in an exhausted heap. Three times per day, the bugaboo can send out a static shock from its bronze sphere. All within 10 feet of the monster suffer 2d6 points of damage (save for half) and have their hair stand up on end.

**Bugaboo: HD 6+1; AC 4 [15]; Atk 2 claws (1d6); Move 15; Save 11; CL/XP 7/600; Special: Fearsome, static shock.**

## Ghul

Ghuls are humans that have acquired a taste for human flesh. Their wickedness and depravity have infused them with a portion of negative energy. Although they remain alive, they can be turned as though undead with 3 extra Hit Dice. A ghul's touch stuns an opponent for one round unless they pass a saving throw. Stunned creatures drop anything they are carrying in their hands and are unable to attack. Although a stunned creature can defend themselves, their opponent receives a +1 bonus to hit them. Ghuls usually fight with a weapon in one gauntleted hand, leaving the other hand empty and bare to make unarmed, potentially stunning attacks. Warriors might wear leather or ring armor, while leaders will wear chainmail or, rarely, platemail. Ghuls can take levels in fighting-man (up to 8th level), magic-user (up to 5th level) and cleric (up to 7th level).

**Ghul: HD 1; AC 6 [13]; Atk 1 weapon (1d8) or one fist (1d2 plus stunning); Move 12; Save 17 (15 vs. spells); CL/XP 2/30; Special: Stunning touch, bonus to save vs. spells.**

## Kruk

Kruks are a tall race of white-skinned humanoids with four arms, duck-like bills and tall, bony crests which allow them to communicate over long distances with rumbling roars. They dwell in subterranean caverns they have carved into perfect squares, with each cavern connected to others via underground canals filled with oily water. Kruks trade humanoid flesh and slaves in markets well attended by other creatures of the underworld.

**Kruk: HD 6+2; AC 5 [14]; Atk 4 slams (1d6); Move 12; Save 11 (6 vs. spells); CL/XP 7/600; Special: +5 save vs. spells.**

## Kyton (Chain Devil)

Kytons look like humanoids wrapped in iron chains with grayish flesh and red eyes showing through the gaps. They can control up to four chains within 20 feet, making them move as they wish. These chains attack as per the kyton, giving the devil up to four extra chain attacks per round. A person holding a chain can make a saving throw to negate the kyton's control over it.

**Kyton: HD 8; AC -1 [20]; Atk 2 chains (1d8+1); Move 12; Save 8; CL/XP 11/1700; Special: Animate chains, +1 or better weapon to hit, magic resistance (40%).**

# Moppe

Moppes are malevolent spirits that inhabit dolls. They cannot move, but they can use the following spells, once per round: *Fear*, *invoke emotion* (save or be possessed by terrible despair or unthinking rage), *hideous laughter* (save or double over laughing for 1d6+1 rounds), *psychic pain* (paralyzed with pain, suffer 1d4 points of intelligence damage and 1d6 points of hit point damage, save for half and to negate the paralysis; for each additional moppe using the power on a victim, the victim suffers an additional -1 penalty to save).

**Moppe: HD 1; AC 11 [8]; Atk none; Move 0; Save 17; CL/XP 3/60; Special: Spells.**

# Night Demon

Night demons are gaunt humanoids with black, rubbery skin, membranous wings sprouting from their shoulders and ankles and a ridge of bumps that runs from their forehead to their tiny, worm-like tail. Any creature seeing a night demon must pass a saving throw or freeze in terror, dropping whatever he is holding. Night demons attack by swooping down on a victim and grabbing them tightly. Once in the nght demon's grasp, the victim is squeezed for 1d4 points of damage per round. Twice per day, a night demon can use *slow* (as the spell) on any creature within sight.

**Night Demon: HD 4; AC 5 [14]; Atk 1 clutch (1d4); Move 9 (Fly 24); Save 13; CL/XP 8/800; Special: Fear aura, slow motion, +1 or better weapon to hit, immunity to cold.**

# Toadstool Man

Toadstool men are misshapen, with mismatched limbs, wide caps colored coral and spotted white and pinched, wrinkled faces with deep, slit mouths. They are like malevolent children, roaming in packs of 3d6 individuals and causing all the havoc they can in the few days in which they have life. Toadstool men emit a poisonous breath that causes all within a cone 10 feet long and 10 feet wide at the base to make a saving throw or suffer 1d6 points of damage. They can breathe this cloud once per day.

**Toadstool Man: HD 3; AC 3 [16]; Atk 1 strike (1d4+1); Move 9; Save 14; CL/XP 4/120; Special: Poison breath, resistance to bludgeoning weapons (50%).**